The Legend of See Bird –
Devil's Backbone

Karl L. Stewart

Publisher Pa[illegible]

an imprint of Headline B[illegible], Inc.

Terra Alta, WV

The Legend of See Bird—Devil's Backbone

by Karl L. Stewart

To order additional copies of this book or for book publishing information, or to contact the author:

Headline Books, Inc.
P.O. Box 52
Terra Alta, WV 26764
www.PublisherPage.com
800-570-5951

Publisher Page is an imprint of Headline Books

ISBN 13: 9781882658282

Library of Congress Control Number: 2015942969

PRINTED IN THE UNITED STATES OF AMERICA

Dedicated to "Granny" Sally Carpenter,
one of the most remarkable women
I have ever known.

Prologue

The cold, grey hand of November lay on the land, smothering the brown wooded ridges and valleys alike in a silent, misty drizzle. The occasional muffled echo of an axe striking wood was all that broke the afternoon silence. Captain Clayton Tibbetts of the 22nd Western Virginia Volunteers, CSA, stood at the make-shift entrance to his dugout, surveying the scene. Dugouts similar and wildly dissimilar to his own dotted the ridge on which his company was deployed. His men had settled in for the long haul, and perhaps that was what was troubling him more than anything.

This was not how 1863 had started. Last spring had been filled with grand speeches and grander expectations. General Robert E. Lee was to lead his unbeaten army of Northern Virginia into combat on the enemy's own ground, to strike hard and fast, to destroy that sluggard McClellan and all his forces, to capture Washington D.C. itself, that nest of vipers, and perhaps, just perhaps, end this war victoriously. Tibbetts' company was to secure this western flank of Lee's army, preparatory to wresting the western counties of Virginia back into the Confederate fold.

But nothing, it seemed, had gone as planned. Captain Tibbetts' chiseled jaw clenched behind his neatly trimmed handlebar moustache as he reflected:

That gorilla Lincoln had sacked McClellan and replaced him with stolid George Meade, and at some worthless village up in Pennsylvania, Gettysburg by name, the goggle-eyed Meade had absorbed and tossed back the best that Lee could throw at him in three days of ferocious fighting. Who would have expected those damned blue-bellies to stand and fight like that? Now, in the late fall of the year, the Confederate army was back where it was last year, several ridges to the east, only in a weaker, more defensive posture as Lee tried to nurse it back to health.

And that wasn't the worst of it. Stonewall Jackson himself was killed in May, and in July the impregnable Vicksburg had fallen to the drunkard Grant and maniac Sherman, slicing the South in two. Now it was impossible to squelch rumors that Grant, who had been placed in charge of the Union forces at Chattanooga, had defeated another Confederate army in what was being called 'the battle above the clouds.' *Yes,* Tibbetts thought, *rumors were flying and it all had taken a terrible toll on his men. Rations were being cut again as the great herds of Texas and western beef were no longer available. Morale was sapped. So many of his men were sick-listed or had deserted that to be truthful his company was no more than a skeleton of itself. And this damnable weather – so cold and wet up in these mountains the men would scarcely drill in it without coercion.* The captain pounded his fist on the door frame in frustration.

But the war was not lost. Surely the cause could not fail. Come spring, he told himself with more conviction than he felt, the Confederacy would rally and drive every last Yankee from the South's sacred soil. Peering into the grey gloom, the Captain was distracted by the approach up the hill of a five man squad. Yes, there could be no doubt about it – the squad was heading directly for him. There could also be no doubt about who was leading it. The tall, dark-haired young man with the long-legged gait was his lieutenant. Tibbetts appreciated his second-in-command more than he liked him. The man rode as though he were born in the saddle and seldom missed what he aimed his rifle at. He had shown both intelligence and a tenacious courage in combat. As a reward, the men bestowed upon him a fearsome nickname and responded well to his leadership. Perhaps that was what bothered the Captain. The men seemed to respect the lieutenant more than they did their captain. Tibbetts had to admit his lieutenant cut an imposing figure, over six feet tall with a broad intelligent forehead. He himself stood barely 5'8", but somehow, standing next to his second in command, he felt even shorter. He turned and retrieved his field hat so as better to meet the approaching squad, and which also added a couple inches to his height.

"Squad, halt!" the tall man barked. He advanced alone to the Captain's dugout. Tibbets met him at the door.

"Yes, Lieutenant, what is it?" He returned the other's salute.

"Sir, these two men were discovered returning to camp. They have been missing for several months. They are Privates Hastings and McCoy." The tall lieutenant seemed to relax just a bit. "Captain, sir, I was wondering what you wanted done with them, seeing as how they returned on their own."

"Yes, I see. I know of these two. Won't you step inside, lieutenant." Tibbetts turned and the lieutenant followed him, leaving the two prisoners and their guards outside. "Be at ease, lieutenant. Would you care for a smoke?" the captain asked.

"No sir, but thank you for offering. Those men are soaked, and I'd as soon get them in out of the weather as I could. There's enough sickness as it is."

"Of course, of course." Tibbetts packed his briar and struck a spark. The small windowless room filled with the pleasant aroma of Virginia tobacco. "What to do with them," he muttered through teeth clenched around the pipe stem. He glanced quickly out the door at the two prisoners now squatting between their guards. "Lieutenant, I know just what to do with those two scoundrels," he snapped. "We are going to make examples of them for the rest of the company. There's a war on, and they have deserted their posts. Heaven knows they are not the only ones, but we are at a crucial point, and the rest of the men have to be made to see that such behavior will not be tolerated. Stonewall Jackson himself shot deserters. I am not quite as bloodthirsty as was our beloved late general, so the prisoners will be hung tomorrow at dawn with the entire company mustered to observe."

The lieutenant removed his hat and ran his fingers nervously through his straight black hair. "But sir, I beg you to reconsider. These are good men who only went home to harvest their crops when we had already taken winter positions up here on this ridge. McCoy's got a young wife who's in the family way, sir, with no one to help her. With all due respect, their families would starve, sir. And the men did come back on their own."

Captain Tibbetts drew in and exhaled a fragrant cloud of pipe smoke. "I appreciate your concern for them. I am sure you know their personal situations better than I. Nonetheless, desertion during time of war is not something to be tolerated. If the other men see military discipline applied, perhaps it will stiffen their spines a bit so when next spring comes around we might still have a company left with some fighting spirit."

"Maybe you're right, sir, but we're already so short of men that I don't see how…"

"That's my job, lieutenant, to see how. Your job is to obey my orders." Tibbetts' voice rose. "Is that perfectly clear?"

Seeing the futility of further argument, the lieutenant stiffened and saluted. "Yes, sir," he said briskly.

Captain Tibbetts, softening a bit said, "Look, lieutenant, I am neither heartless nor stupid. I know Private Hastings is your cousin, but I also know that McCoy's brother, Harmon, currently serves in the Union army. And when this man deserts, suspicion of his commitment to the cause is warranted. As for your cousin, surely you can see that I cannot play favorites." Seeing the unmoved face before him, the captain averted his gaze and said tersely, "We are on the brink of losing this company. I expect you and all the men under my command to follow lawful orders. I also expect you to see to it that the prisoners are informed of my decision. Make arrangements with the parson if the condemned so wish, and prepare for those two deserters," he jabbed his finger toward the door, "to be hung at dawn. That is all." He saluted dismissal and turned his back to his subordinate.

There was a stifled comment, a rustle at the door, and then silence. When Captain Tibbetts turned, he was alone again in his dugout. The five others had disappeared.

The company stockade was another dugout, much like the captain's. Two sides were dug into the side of the ridge. Two sides were composed of stout logs. The only window was a small one cut into the rough-cut door. The whole thing was covered with heavy timbers and coarse shingles. A crooked, rusty pipe served as a chimney, from which flowed a thin ribbon of smoke which lingered indecisively before crawling off toward the ridge line. Now late in the afternoon a single guard stood beside the door in the evening gloom. The thoroughly miserable lieutenant approached the guard, who when he recognized him, stood aside. "Good evening, lieutenant."

"That is certainly debatable, Private Jenkins. Jenkins it is, isn't it? You hail from over by the Kanawha valley, don't you?"

"Yes, sir. All my kin are still there, 'cept those who're dead or gone to the hills, fighting the Yankees ranger style."

The lieutenant paused a moment, sizing up the guard. "Private Jenkins," he spoke quietly, "why don't you step inside with me while I talk to the prisoners. I have an idea I'd like to present to you and those two men."

"Of course, sir. If you don't mind my saying so, most of the rest of the men think it's a cryin' shame those fellers gotta die for what they did. There ain't a man amongst them what wouldn't have done the same. 'Cept most of them wouldn't have come back." He took a step backwards. "After you, sir."

Jenkins unbolted and opened the door, and the lieutenant ducked to step inside. Hastings and McCoy rose to their feet. McCoy spoke first. "Is it true they're gonna stretch our necks come dawn, Anderson?"

"'Fraid so. That is the Captain's intention. But before you boys throw in the towel, I've got me an idea that may just benefit the Confederacy without clipping our own ranks. You boys interested? If so hear me out. Jenkins, sit yourself down by the fire there and listen, too. You know those blue bellies have claimed the western half of Virginia and hold it by force. Hell, with most of the fighting men gone, who could stop them? Well, I'm proposing the four of us bug out tonight for parts west. We can keep an eye on our families and at the same time make it pretty hot for those Yankees. We can form up an informal unit, maybe join up with the border ranger outfit operating there. We'll hit the Yankees hard and fast and then melt into the hills." He struck a hand with a fist for emphasis. "We know that area like the back of our hands." The men leaned forward, nodding their agreement. "They'll never find us, and we can do a whole lot more for the South by fighting ranger style then by sitting here and rotting all winter. We've little time for long-winded debate. So I'm calling for a straight up vote. What do you say?"

The only sound was the soft crackling of the fire. The men looked from face to face, gauging sentiment.

McCoy spoke first. A handsome man, he stood, straightened his lithe frame and reached out his right hand. "Anderson, that's the most decent thing any man has ever done for me and way more than I expected. All I really got in this world is my family. You're giving me a chance to protect and fight for them. I ain't never gonna forget it." The lieutenant shook his hand and as he did so the others stood and shook his hand in turn.

"We'll have to move fast," he said. "I've got us some horses ready for a night patrol just in case you boys saw it my way. Jenkins, you fetch them. Say the night patrol needs them. I'll leave here first and we'll all meet down by the stream in one hour. We disappear tonight. I figure in this murk Tibbetts won't be able to do a blamed thing about it. But we need to leave tonight." He scanned the small group. "Ready, boys?" The tension was palpable.

Private Hastings spoke, "What are we standing here for? We're with you, Devil Anse." The tall lieutenant smiled grimly and exited quickly. Several minutes later, into the twilight drizzle stepped the three mountaineers. Like specters, with not a sound, they melted into the shadows.

1

See Bird Carpenter strained against the weight of the large timber he, with the help of a horse, a rope and a pulley, was hoisting into place on the wall he was erecting. The timber, gently lowered into place three rows above the door, ran the length of the house. Slacking off the rope slightly, he jumped up on the wagon bed and gave the dove-tailed end a whack with a mallet, locking it into the row below. Then, unhitching the rope, he stood back to admire his work. With the placement of the final timber, the exterior walls of the house were completed.

He stroked the broad neck of the horse in affection, and it whinnied gently in return, acknowledging his attention. When he sent for Kiamichi he really did not know what to expect. Left behind with his good friend and rancher Luke Strebow when See Bird came east, the big horse had been his constant companion for years as he made the rounds of the rodeos springing up everywhere west of the Mississippi. Would Kiamichi remember him? Would he forgive the man for leaving him behind? Would he be so upset with all the train travel he endured that he would be worthless or even dangerous with rage? See Bird need not have worried. When Kiamichi was unloaded at the C & O rail yard in Huntington, after a brief adjustment period he settled down wonderfully, and when See Bird clicked his tongue the way he had a thousand times before, the big horse flicked his ears in recognition and pranced over to the man who tamed him, resting his muzzle on his shoulder. It was enough to bring tears to even the most stoic observer.

Now that he had settled down to the life of a 'farmer' here in West Virginia, he intended to purchase several more horses as deals would make them available. But first for the roof and the long porch he was planning. He frowned as his critical eye detected a slight bow in one of the timbers on a side wall. But he decided he'd be hanged before he would disassemble the wall to replace or turn one timber. *Besides*, he thought, *once the whole thing was properly caulked no one would notice one slightly less than perfect timber.* He smiled to himself because he knew the lie even as he thought it – that bent log would bother him every time he saw it – for the rest of his life.

Hopping down, the young Choctaw doffed the uncreased black slouch hat he nearly always wore and used it to broom the wood chips off his denims. Sweat ran in rivulets down his hard copper-colored body. Never a big man, he had learned to use his brains to make up for his lack of size. Even so, his 5'6" frame carried a rock solid 140 pounds. Many times over the years, larger men, underestimating him, had called him out and consequently paid the price.

Years of working on western ranches had made See Bird an independent, self-sufficient man, perhaps not gifted with his tongue, but blessed with an unexplainable power that flowed through his hands. When he reflected on it, he could not make up his mind as to whether it was a gift or a curse. His abilities became apparent within a short time of his arrival in the bustling new city of Huntington, established as a railroad terminus by the railroad magnate Collis P. Huntington, and people sought him out from miles around for blacksmithing, leather and wood work. There was so much work coming his way, he discovered, that with his shop work and construction of the farm buildings he was left with precious little time to court the young widow Sally Osbourne.

He loved thinking about her with her flaxen hair, large brown eyes deep enough to swallow a man whole, and her in-your-face directness and honesty. As he settled down in the shade of a big cottonwood to eat the lunch she had packed, he realized he loved just about everything about her. He bought this farm with the stake he had earned rodeoing and working the west, and she decided to pitch her lot in with him as well. The result – he built a lean-to for his temporary accommodations, and lived on the land he owned when he wasn't in town. Sally lived in Huntington on Monroe Avenue, a good day's buggy ride from the farm, taking in laundry and sewing and tending to little Gertrude, her three year old daughter by her former husband, a sheriff who had been shot dead trying to serve a warrant on moonshiners. With See Bird's help she had turned a new leaf and no longer worked down on Frog Island as a dolly. She did what she had because it was better than starving, but she was very proud of her status as a new-made woman.

See Bird bit into a crisp apple and looked around. Yes, sir, this was a mighty fine land, even though it had more than its share of red clay, and was hillier than almost any place he'd ever been, even the old family homestead in south-east Oklahoma. Yet already it felt more like home. Sally spent the previous night with some kin down the road and this morning paid a surprise visit, bringing in his food. A dead-eyed shot with his Winchester, he really wasn't lacking much with the woods full of game and berries ripening fast. Still, after a bit of showing her what he had accomplished and sharing a few tender minutes he sent her on her way again, telling her that she was not to come out here anymore until he was finished and the house ready for them to move into. She stood there, lips tight, hands on her narrow hips, and even squinted up her eyes like she was angry. But she held her tongue, and when he held her by the shoulders and kissed her forehead, they both burst out laughing, evaporating whatever tension she had been feeling. He had a few surprises planned for her and didn't want her to come waltzing in unexpectedly, spoiling his fun. *As a matter of fact,* he thought, *now would be a good time to get busy on that indoor plumbing. It would take a couple days, but there was no reason it couldn't be done. And she would really like it.* His thoughts were interrupted as he heard a buggy rattling up the trail and hoped it wasn't her again.

He didn't recognize the stranger, but there was no mistaking the 30.06 resting on the seat next to him. There was nothing about the man to indicate his visit was anything other than friendly, yet See Bird felt uneasy and glanced around. "Howdy, neighbor," he said. "What can I do for you?" and took a step towards the stranger.

The buggy driver carefully placed the reins down and leaned back on the wagon bench, tipping his derby hat to the back of his head, a smile plastered on his face - a very picture of studied informality. But See Bird also caught the coldness in the man's eyes that belied the smile on his mouth. The stranger studied See Bird's handiwork. What he did not seem to take notice of was the lack of an invitation to step down. See Bird knew well the rule of the West that no man would set foot on another's property without being invited. He presumed it was the same here. "How do, friend," the man in the buggy answered as he leaned over the side and spat a stream of tobacco into the grass. Seeing See Bird's hesitation he pulled aside a corner of his soiled vest, revealing a tin star pinned to his shirt. "I'm the law from over in Pikeville." He smiled again, but it never reached his ice-cold steel-grey eyes.

See Bird cocked his head. "Excuse me for saying, but isn't it a bit odd for a Kentucky lawman to be prowling the hills over here in West Virginia?" A complete silence descended on the clearing.

"Might be so, but I'm here to take in a desperado named Tom Wallace for murder. You ain't happened to have seen him now, have you?"

"Might be I have. Folks have stopped by now and again. But the name don't ring a bell." He tossed his apple core toward the edge of the silent woods and then looked directly at his visitor. "Mostly when folks come by they don't hide in the trees. If you want to continue this little parley, call in your boys." See Bird backed up a couple steps closer to the Winchester leaning against his wagon wheel.

"Now don't go getting' antsy, mister." The Kentucky lawman held up one hand. "It's just that a man has to be careful. He never knows what he might be stepping into." See Bird was silent, but stopped within reach of his rifle. The lawman in the buggy turned his body and called out, "It's okay. Come on in, men." From out of the shadows, three men carrying rifles stepped their horses forward to flank the wagon. "These are my deputies. I'm the Pike County sheriff, Coburn by name. We got off on the wrong foot, and I apologize for that."

The insinuating smile returned to his face. "Fact is, you got no law over here – least ways none that will do anything about the murdering outlaws that run and hide in these hills."

See Bird didn't take the bait to introduce himself. Instead, he casually picked up his Winchester and cradled it in his arms. He figured the odds had now shifted into his favor. "First place, what you say is true. We did get off on the wrong foot. But men who sneak up on others in the woods and then flash a tin star from somewhere else got no rights I'm aware of to ask anyone anything. Might be this Wallace is a coward and murderer, like you say. Might be he ain't. I don't rightly care." He raised his rifle, swinging it slightly forward, menacingly, but with his finger still off the trigger, his body loose. "Now I got a lot of work to do, and I ain't going to waste one more minute of the day on the likes of you. So long now, and I don't expect I'll be seeing you boys again."

Two of the men on horseback slouched in their saddles, one wearing a wide, blank-faced grin displaying a number of missing or rotten teeth, the hawk-nosed man next to him sullen and still. See Bird felt if trouble came, it would be from the third man, sitting his horse stiff-backed on the other side of the wagon, lightly holding the reins in his left hand while resting his gun hand on his thigh, looking eager to start the dance. The sheriff spoke, "Okay boys, let's head out. It's clear this man can't help us." As he picked up the reins he spoke to See Bird, "Mister, one thing is for sure. You got grit, standing up to four armed men, and I respect you for it. Just watch out who you associate with. Looks like you're building a home for a family here, maybe wife and kids. I hope things work out for you but it sure would be a shame if they was to get hurt somehow 'cause you was to cross the wrong man."

See Bird's voice lowered to a steely whisper, "Is that a threat?" His grip on the rifle tightened.

"Not at all, not at all. Just a friendly warning. Good day to you." He flicked the reins of the buggy and started away. His posse fell in behind.

See Bird watched and listened until he could hear them no more. A pair of crows nearby laughed raucously. But he couldn't shake the uneasy feeling in the pit of his stomach.

Patting the neck of his horse he said, "Well, big fella, that was a close call. But we still got us a house to build. He put the Winchester down and picked up the mallet."

2

Sally stood before the looking glass, wondering at the apparition in azure staring back at her, and wondering also at her great good fortune. A little over a month ago she was working the Huntington boat landing picking up whatever money she could by doing whatever she could to please strange men. More than once over that time she had held little Gertrude in her arms and watched the big river flow past, miserably considering putting an end to it all, only to step back, as if called by the sad dark eyes of her little one.

As though waking from long a nightmare, she had to pinch herself to be certain it was all real. She met a man, a man who loved her for herself and who she could be, not for what she used to be, a man who planned for the future, not one who lived in the past. He came from the West and maybe that's what the West does to a person. Sally was not much of a believer, but when See Bird proposed to her, knowing full well her sordid past, and proposed his plan for their future together, she burst into tears of joy and thankfulness, and that night as she tucked her daughter in she knelt by the little bed and sent up fireworks of prayer thanking the God who had brought this turnabout in her life.

Hearing the door to the parlor open, she turned to see her Aunt Lily bustle in, clucking and carrying on so much like a hen, Sally laughed inwardly at the thought. The two women met in an embrace and locked arms . "Are you ready, Sally?" The bride could only nod. "All right then, let's go. Preacher Anse is waiting." Taking Sally in tow, she pivoted as her sister Dreana struck up a familiar hymn on the upright piano in the parlor. "You know John always likes me to call him 'Preacher Anse' in public. He and his cousin 'Devil Anse' are as different as night and day and yet as stubbornly alike as two peas in a pod. Mercy me. Listen to me rattle on. Preacher says my tongue wags at both ends. Take a deep breath down your goosal pipe now, girl." She paused and breathed deeply herself. "Someone's waiting for you out there, and mercy me, does he ever look fine."

It was a simple ceremony, performed by Preacher Anse Hatfield in the Hardshell Baptist Church, witnessed by his wife Lily and her sister Dreana. Gertrude sat next to Dreana on the piano bench, watching the woman's fingers intently and kicking her dangling legs in time with the music. The unexpected guest wearing a full beard parted in the middle was Preacher's more famous or notorious cousin Devil Anse, just over 50 years old, and the undisputed patriarch of the largest clan in the Tug Fork area. He beamed with pride at his niece, Sally. Following the "I do's" he stepped over to the young couple, and after glancing about for prying eyes, produced a flask of an amber liquid, certainly not coffee, from the inside pocket of his houndstooth waistcoat. After taking a swig, he introduced himself to See Bird. "Young man, he said, "I want you to know you have just married one of the finest and most beautiful women within a hundred miles." Sally, unused to flattery or compliments, felt the unfamiliar sensation of embarrassment creeping over her. "She probably has not told you I'm the person who taught her how to ride and shoot when she was but a mite of a girl, and her sticks," he gestured to her legs, "were so skinny I wondered how she'd ever sit a horse."

At this reference to her body, Sally began to blush furiously. "Uncle Devil Anse, please." She lifted her chin, set her face into what she hoped was a look of scornful disdain, and said imperiously, "If you men would excuse me, I just remembered something I need to tell Aunt Lucy," She then spun away in a fragrant blue cloud that left both men staring and smiling for a few seconds. Devil Anse picked up his train of thought.

"But don't let that tiny form fool you. Sally is as tough as they come. She's dealt with more hard knocks in her short life than any two other women twice her age. Might be she can't read a word, but take my word for it, that gal ain't nobody's fool. I'm sure she'll share the gory details with you as you gain her trust. So I'm not worried about her. And I've seen some of your work, and heard about some more. I figure you for a straight shooter and a man of your word. But sometimes the world can sort of gang up on a man. I'm speaking here from experience. I know you are a wary man, and that ought to keep you healthy. There was trouble a few years back during an election. My brother Ellison was murdered by Ran'l McCoy and three of his sons. They stabbed him twenty-six times and shot him in the back. We hunted his sons down and killed them for what they done." The big man looked See Bird in the eye and added, "They got only what they had comin' to them, but it set their pa off, and he ain't been the same since. He's sent a lot of bad characters to prowl these hills looking for Hatfields to hunt and hurt. They'll find you. Make sure they don't peg you for the runt of the litter sucking at the hind teat. But if you find yourself in a tight place, I want you to know there is nothing, not religion, not government, not even the law, that's stronger than family. Feel free to call on me if you ever need help."

"Mr. Hatfield…" See Bird started before he was interrupted.

"Devil Anse will do fine, See Bird. I kind of took to that name." He took another surreptitious gulp of the whiskey from his flask. "It kind of backs people off and gives me some breathin' room. And if you don't want folks crowding you, might be you'll choose to answer to another name.

"Devil Anse then," See Bird continued, "I appreciate your concern for Sally and you're accepting me in your family. To the people I come from family is also important, but I've always liked my space too. Anybody who hurts either of those two," nodding to Sally and Gertrude over at the piano, "will live only long enough to regret it. As for my name, most folks round here know me as 'Red.' I'm comfortable with that." He paused for a moment as if considering his next words. Then he continued, "I do have one question that maybe you can help me with. I came to this place partly because I heard my twin brother may have traveled this way a few years back. They say he looks a lot like me. Goes by the name, See Right. I would kindly appreciate it if you hear anything about him to let me know."

Devil Anse considered this request for a moment. "A twin brother," he repeated thoughtfully and stroked the right half of his beard absentmindedly. "I'll tell you what, Red. I'll ask around. You're in a big family now, and not much passes through these hills without some kin seeing it. If he's been through here in the last five years, I'll find out. But for now, I think your bride and daughter are waiting." See Bird turned his head only to meet Sally's serene gaze directly. Little Gertrude, in high buttoned shoes and a fluffy calico dress Sally had made special for the occasion, was skipping circles around her mother, singing a nonsense rhyme she was spontaneously composing.

"You're right. We've a long haul to make before we get home tonight, and we'd best be on our way." The two men shook hands in parting as Preacher Anse was approaching.

"Well now, Red," he said, "I hope this is not the last we see of you in church until your funeral." They shook hands as well.

"Preacher, thank you for what you done," he rejoined. "As for whether or not you see much of us, that'll be pretty much up to the lady in blue over there. But we'll try."

"And what about you, Devil Anse? Am I ever going to see you in this building again other than in a coffin?" Preacher ribbed his cousin. But if he expected Devil Anse to be embarrassed, he was surprised by the response.

"Coz, I'll tell you what," Devil Anse said and placed one hand on Preacher's shoulder, "I belong to no church unless you say I belong to the one great Church of the world." He wouldn't let Preacher Anse interrupt. Perhaps the whiskey had lubricated his tongue a bit. He continued, "If you like, you can say it is the devil's church I belong to."

The good pastor just shook his head at the blasphemy. "It's my own fault for bringing it up, but just the same, I'll be praying for your soul, brother, and who knows, maybe one of these days I'll have me the opportunity of baptizing the Devil himself." He smiled at his joke and turned to walk away.

"Take care, Red." Devil Anse said in parting. "Ride safe." With that, See Bird collected his new family, said quick goodbyes, and climbed aboard the buggy, which had been packed with a beautiful counterpane, hand-stitched by sisters Lily and Dreana, jars of jellies and currants and pickles and whatever else might make starting out a new married life just a bit sweeter.

It was near dusk when the wagon and its passengers - two very tired adults and one small child sound asleep on some bedding in the back, rounded a bend and ascended a small rise which dropped into another hollow through which ran a small stream that fed into a bigger creek, which in turn deposited the accumulated water into the Tug Fork. In turn, the Tug Fork joined the Louisa, forming the Big Sandy, which carried all the waters of these hills to the mighty Ohio. But it was not these thoughts that brought a gasp from Sally. Nor were they the reason she reached over and clutched See Bird's hand. There, before her and slightly below, nestled among cottonwoods and oak, sat a lovely timbered house with a long low-slung porch running its length. The last of the evening's golden rays bathed the whole scene in their soft glow and reflected off the windows, making the whole seem lighted from within.

See Bird, mistaking her reaction to the sight, began, "I know it ain't much, Sal. Everything's still pretty fresh. It needs your touch, curtains and…"

"Shut up, you foolish man," she cut him off gently. "I never seen anything so beautiful in all my born days. And I don't expect I ever will. Dear See Bird…" She looked up into his eyes and saw them worried and questioning. Overwhelmed by emotion, tears flowed unchecked down her cheeks. Leaning over, See Bird's lips met hers in a kiss that promised forever, tender yet hungry. They sat there like that, his arm around her shoulders, her head resting against him, lost in their own silent thoughts, until the first stars appeared.

Slowly then, they made their way down to the house in Warm Hollow where their new life would begin.

Over the next several days, life on "the farm" as they called it, began to take on a routine. With so much to be done, a division of labor quickly emerged: Anything that had to do with the inside of the house, from the arrangement of furniture to cooking, sewing or cleaning, was clearly Sally's domain. Her word was law – See Bird learned that on the second day, when during a sudden summer deluge, she met him at the door with his moccasins in hand and would not allow him in with muddy boots. When he entered he was wearing his mocs and his boots stayed on the porch. Everything outside was his responsibility. Gertrude dwelt equally well in both worlds: Indeed she seemed to feel that whether it was boiling beans or building a barn, her advice was essential and she did not hesitate for a second to give 'Pap', as she called See Bird, the benefit of her nearly four years experience.

One morning as See Bird was stacking a pile of rails and posts for a fence to contain the animals which had yet to appear, two men rode in on a wagon filled with rattling tools. See Bird hailed them and invited them down. Hearing the wagon approach, Sally stepped to the door and, waving a dish towel, called to one of the men. "Cap, you Cap Hatfield, what are you doing down here? I know you didn't come to work, now did you?"

"Hey, Sal," he rejoined. "Pa said as how it's a light lumber day, maybe Jim and me could help out a bit." See Bird approached with a smile. "And you must be Red. Pa said you were building this farm alone and could maybe use a hand. Appears to me you got a stack of palings over there what need some man-handling."

See Bird offered his hand to both men and led them over to the stack of rails. "Well, I never asked for help but I sure won't turn the offer down. It's neighborly of you to offer. Here's what we got to do…" Together, the three men pitched right in, stopping for a break only when Sally brought out a pot of coffee and some mugs. See Bird had to admit to himself that Cap and Jim were men who could work with him step for step, and his respect for them grew accordingly. "Actually," Cap said as he tossed out the dregs of his coffee, "this is kind of a break for us. Most days we're up for breakfast at four and lumbering as soon's it gets light." He paused and then continued, "Besides, Pa thought it might be good for us to make ourselves scarce for a while."

Seeing See Bird's puzzled expression, Jim added, "Rumor is there's a Kentucky posse headed this way to try to take us in for a gunfight that happened over at Ran'l McCoy's place. He's been plaguing us for so long it just seemed best we should take the fight to him. He got away, but a son and a girl of his died in the shooting. I'm right sorry it happened that way," he said contritely, "but we wanted to be able to sleep at home beside better bed fellows than Winchester rifles, and once in a while to be able to take our boots off when we go to bed." Here Jim stopped and averted his gaze. Cap said nothing more. As they rose to continue their work See Bird wondered what exactly he had gotten himself into.

That evening, after a meal of pinto beans and ham, collards and hot cornbread slathered in butter, all washed down by pots of fresh coffee, Sally topped it all serving up huge slabs of wild berry pie. While she cleaned up with Gertrude's 'help', the men retreated to the porch to talk some more and admire the rail fences they had installed around several acres of land that would be the corral, the smaller barnyard, and the even smaller one around the shed that was designated for swine. See Bird picked up a chunk of wood and after examining it for a minute, set to work on it with a big knife he wore on his belt. "Boys," he began, "Sal and I really appreciate you throwing in with us today. The Good Lord knows there's plenty enough to do. If you've a mind to, tomorrow's got a load of work on its own, finishing up the shed door and gates. You're welcome to bunk on mats in the house. You know Sal will feed you as much as you can eat. But before you agree, there's one thing I gotta know." He paused and rotated the piece of wood as if looking for a way in and then continued. "In my time I've had to fight and even kill some men. And I never lost a minute's sleep over it. And I don't mean to stick my nose where it don't belong, but the other day I was visited by four hard cases. Now you're telling me there was a fight and a woman was killed. If you tell me you had nothing to do with it, well then I'm much obliged, and I'll back your play. But if you killed a woman, and now you turn the eyes of those bounty hunters my direction, and if my woman gets hurt, there will be hell to pay. So which is it?" He carefully laid the wood and the knife down beside him and, folding his hands, waited for a response.

Cap spoke. "Red, it's only because you're family that I'll explain myself. If you was anybody else, those could be fighting words you just spoke." See Bird nodded but remained silent. The only sound was Sally's muffled voice talking quietly to Gertrude as she prepared her for bed. Devil Anse's second son continued, "For years, since the election where three McCoys were killed, things quieted down. Now it seems something's stirred up the hornet's nest again. Pa's tried to avoid trouble. He's sold off land and moved farther back in the hills. He even wrote a letter offering peace and a dollar settlement of the issue. But McCoy spits on him and now has these hills crawling with his blood suckers. It's got so we can't even cut trees without us going armed. Even the Preacher has been shot at." Here Cap hunched his shoulders a bit, and his voice seemed less truculent. "Okay, so a while ago me and about a dozen of the boys decided to end it once and for all. We surrounded McCoy's place at night and told the old man to come out. They started firing at us and so we let them have it. We didn't know who all was inside, and someone jumped up on the roof and set the place on fire to flush them out. Ran'l got away in the dark, but a daughter and son didn't. All in all, it was a mess. But I swear, neither of us did it. The thought of a wounded girl in that burning house still makes my guts roil."

"Fighting at night is the worst kind," See Bird said. "Things go wrong in a hurry. And you can't make them right. I believe you, Cap. But you know you boys will have to have your day in court, else this feuding and killing will go on forever."

"Red," Jim Vance spoke up, "What you say is the Bible truth, but the truth also is that if we surrender to McCoy's crew we will never make it to the jail alive. And then what'll Pa do? Things will just get worse."

There appeared to the trio on the porch no way out of the cycle of violence. See Bird retrieved his knife and wood chunk, and they sat in silence for a while as he carved. Finally, he spoke, "There is one way as I see it, to maybe settle accounts. Cap, you tell your pa to send someone down here once in a while to keep an eye on things for a few days, and the three of us will hike on over to Pikeville. No horses. These woods are too close, too easy to set up an ambush. Pikeville's the last place on earth this crew will be looking for you, and since no one knows me from Adam's off-ox, I can trace out the safe paths for us. What do you say? Are you willing to give it a try?"

The two men grunted as if gut-punched. Cap picked his teeth with a splinter for a minute. Jim sat staring at his feet. See Bird gave the two men as much time as they needed to consider their position. Cap finally broke the silence. "Red, when we rode in this morning I didn't know what to expect. Sally's had her some bad luck with men." He extended his right hand. "But she hit the jackpot with you. I'm willing to do what you say. This warring can't go on forever. What do you say, Jim? I'll swing by your place to meet up with you, we'll hike down here and go in together."

His companion finally nodded reluctantly and looked up at the other two men, "I'm not sure we couldn't finish this off ourselves with just one big push, like we tried before. But, yep, count me in. Only we got to get going soon. I don't think we can dodge them coyotes forever. Let's hang them barn doors and gates in the morning, then we'll head home to collect some gear and say our goodbyes."

See Bird looked at the two grim men on the porch. *If this worked out*, he thought, *it would go a long way toward bringing peace to these hills. One thing for sure, it took more than just a little bit of courage to make the decision these two men just had.* "Since my place is closest to Pikeville, why don't we all meet here day after tomorrow?" The men nodded their assent.

The screen door opened and Sally stepped out. "She's already asleep, the little sweet pea," she said. "Would you men like a cup of fresh perked coffee or another piece of pie?"

Cap perked right up, "I don't care if I do. The coffee sure does smell good."

"Sally," See Bird said as he swooped her into his arms, "if you keep up this way, I'm going to end up a fat little roly-poly man."

"Least that way," she retorted, "I'd have me something to grab on to," and bussed him square on his lips, leaving him stunned into silence while his guests hooted good-naturedly.

"Well, Mary, looks like this is goodbye for a while." Jim Vance picked up his battered hat and wobbled toward the door to his small timbered home in the woods. "Cap's waiting outside, and we got to get down to Red's place."

Mary looked distressed and compulsively wiped her hands on her apron. "Maybe you ought to put it off a day or two. I don't think that possum is sitting too well with you. You'd feel better tomorrow morning."

Jim rubbed his growling stomach and grimaced. "I do believe you are right about that," he said miserably. "I been spending more time in the outhouse than in the house, but this is what we all planned, and I've got to point one foot in the right direction or I might back down and never get up the gumption again to do it. And my stomach, it'll settle down in a while." He tried a smile, but it faded before it bloomed as another wave of nausea threatened to overwhelm him.

"Oh, Jimmy," Mary pleaded, "At least let me walk with you two down to Sally's. I ain't seen her in a month of Sundays - we could have us a nice chat." Sensing his hesitation, she added, "And besides, this woods is crawling with bounty hunters. I could walk on ahead and sort of scout it out for you two." She wore such a pleading face and her misery and worry were so obvious, the combination caved in Jim's resistance.

"All right then," he conceded, "I guess it would be a good thing for you to visit Sally. It might be a good idea even if you was to spend a day or so there until Red gets back. "Seeing her relief he added, "So what're you waiting for? Grab your bonnet. Let's go."

The trio then started down the trail toward Warm Hollow. True to her intention to scout the road ahead, Mary led the men by about a hundred feet, enjoying the stroll, listening to the sighing breeze rustle the forest canopy far above. The walk proceeded more slowly than they expected in order to accommodate Jim's need for frequent roadside breaks caused by the tainted possum. During such a pause, Mary stepped round a curve in the trail only to come face to face with Coburn and his three 'deputies' on foot. Instantly sizing up the situation, she turned and began running back toward Jim and Cap. "Run, Jimmy. They're here." A pistol butt smashed into her skull, sending her sprawling as pain cascaded through her head. The four men cursed her as they raced past. Cap fired off a few ineffectual rounds in their direction and then dodged into the thick undergrowth, driven off by the volley of return fire from the charging group of men.

Jim found himself in an especially exposed position, still tugging up his trousers as Coburn and his men cornered him, his pistol lying on the ground beside him. "Don't shoot. I surren…," was all he said before a bullet to his gut slammed him to the ground. A wicked smile on his face and a smoking gun in his hand, Coburn walked up to Jim, now pushing himself up to a kneeling position. "We was headed into Pikeville to turn ourselves in," he said.

"Well, I'm mighty glad we got here when we did then, Jim Vance. Too bad the other one run off, but I guess I'll collect the bounty on you at least." He leveled the pistol at the back of Jim's head and squeezed the trigger, sending the lifeless corpse sprawling. "Boys, that's one more rat wiped out. But I won't get my money if I don't have the evidence." He holstered his gun, knelt over the bloody corpse and unsheathed his knife.

See Bird heard the high-pitched screaming before he could determine its source. He was finishing up the installation of a latch on the shed door, and at first thought it must be coming from the house. He looked in that direction but all he saw was Gertrude marching along the porch, singing to herself, and tapping the planks with a stick in time to her song. Another burst of hysterical wailing, this time closer, brought her to a standstill. As if frozen in place she stared toward the woods. See Bird swung that way as well.

What he saw galvanized him into action. A woman stumbled out of the woods and nearly fell. She gathered herself and shrieked again while tearing at her blood-smeared hair. "Sally," See Bird yelled as he raced toward the distraught woman, "take Gertrude inside – now!" Appearing at the door, the small child's mother scooped her up and disappeared inside, slamming the door. See Bird reached Mary just as she was collapsing and, catching her, gently lowered her to the ground. Seeing the nasty welt on her head and the gash that left her hair matted with blood, he asked her insistently, "Mary, who did this to you?" She responded by breaking into uncontrollable sobs and clutching at his shirt with her gory hands. "Please, Mary, tell me what happened to you."

"Oh, God, them devils. They came a'hunting for us."

Hearing her hysterical words, See Bird tried to calm her down. "It's going to be all right now. But you got to tell me who hurt you."

"Me?" her eyes finally focused on him. "It ain't me, Red, cain't you hear?" she sobbed. "Them devils done shot and scalped my Jimmy – shot and scalped him."

3

Word raced on the backs of fast horses from hollow to hollow throughout the Tug Fork watershed, and within a short time grim-faced, well armed men began arriving at Devil Anse's home for the council of war. Anderson Hatfield, known to everyone but his wife Levicy as Devil Anse, had built this place primarily for defense. His family living-quarters —a large two-room cabin, not very different from any other cabin one might see in this part of Appalachia. But where it was situated was unique: Feeling vulnerable during the early days of the feud, he sold off some 5,000 acres of land elsewhere and bought two parcels of land, comprising nearly 500 acres, back here in the mountains. He built his new home in a narrow valley, a cove, between two ridges that extended down the east side of the highest mountain between Logan, West Virginia, and the Kentucky border along Island Creek, a stream that fed into the Guyandotte River. The location was so isolated that unless a person had business there, he would instinctively avoid it. And it would be impossible to approach it unobserved.

Nearby, he built a fort in case someone would ever try to take him by force. Walls constructed of 12" thick oak with a door to match – the only entrance – would easily absorb or deflect heavy fire. Gun ports in each wall were cut to provide overlapping fields of fire kept clear by the removal of trees and brush from the fort's vicinity. The entire place was kept stocked with canned food, fresh water, and a plentiful supply of fuel for the massive stone fireplace.

The immediate neighborhood was comprised almost completely of Hatfield partisans, folks who kept a wary watch for the approach of possibly hostile strangers. That did not mean Devil Anse was inhospitable. In truth, he was a sociable man with a reputation for fairness, who loved good fiddle music, good company, and good whiskey. But on this occasion another trait emerged. He, like the rest of his clan and indeed, like the McCoys as well, were proud and intolerant of insult or injury. When pushed, they pushed back hard.

As nearly a hundred men and a considerable number of women and children assembled in the fort, stacking their arms at the door, they stood about, sharing the news and wondering what Devil Anse was going to say. But the first to speak was Cap. See Bird watched the auburn-haired man and listened as he related the ambush in detail, right down to the gory description of Jim Vance's execution-style murder and scalping. The room was so quiet in the telling that the men in the rear had no trouble hearing. As Cap wrapped it up, See Bird noticed a crackling murmur of electric tension filling the room.

After a few seconds' hesitation Devil Anse rose from a bench where he sat along one side wall and strode to the front of the room. The patriarch of the clan made an undeniable impression. A lifetime of hard work told in his powerful frame, broad shoulders, and deep chest. Clad in a faded blue long-sleeved shirt, open at the collar, and blue jeans tucked into his high boots, and with a large colt strapped to his waist, he gazed at the assembled clan like an eagle, See Bird thought, his dark brown eyes crowned by thick black eyebrows, beak-like nose, and mass of jet black hair combed back from a widow's peak. *If it was true, as Sally had told him, the Hatfields emigrated from the Scottish Highlands, there was no doubt the man standing at the front of this room would have been as equally at home amid the skirling bagpipes, leading kilted warriors into battle as he was here, in the highlands of West Virginia. His charismatic presence engendered trust and respect. What would the man say?* Even the quiet whispering in the large room stilled as all eyes focused on their leader, each man wondering the same thing.

"Folks," he began, "you've all heard what happened. And you all know why it happened - a night raid on somebody's home where an innocent person was killed. My son and Jim knew they done wrong for it and was trying to surrender." He paused momentarily. "They weren't given the chance. Now we gotta do something or be hunted down and murdered, too. Else we ain't worth this here handful of salt." He opened a clenched fist and slowly poured the salt it held onto the floor.

"Let's clean out all them McCoys once and for all!" someone shouted. Others loudly agreed.

Devil Anse raised his hand and waited for the noise to subside before continuing. "We could do that, ain't no doubt about it. But then what?" He paused a few seconds to let the question sink in before continuing. "And then we'd all be arrested or killed, and our womenfolk and kids would be all alone. Is that what you want?"

"You tell us then what else we can do," another man shouted. "You said yourself we cain't just ignore it."

"There's a couple things we need to do, Charley," he continued. "We got to make sure something like this don't happen again. These hills are infested with hawkshaws, just like Coburn and his crew. Kentucky put money on our heads, and that makes us marked men." He ran a hand through his hair again. "They even want $500 for my hair." He smiled, "But I do believe it's worth more than that to me. So I think I'll just keep it a bit longer." The tension eased slightly as a few men chuckled. Then Devil Anse stepped over to face the wall he had been sitting against at the start of the meeting and said, "Now look you men over here." A bed sheet suspended at two corners hung on it. "This here is a map I drew of the area. The 'X' right here is this fort. Over here is the Tug Fork, and you can see how it meets the Louisa and goes into the Big Sandy and the whole mess flows into the Ohio at Cattlettsburg."

"But what's all them spots and squiggly lines for?" someone called out.

"And how come you got the Big Sandy climbing the wall? Shouldn't it go sideways, if you know what I mean?" a man protested. Others told the two to hold their tongues, but Devil Anse, after glaring at the questioners for a moment, smiled and shook his head. Then he calmly unpinned the bed sheet and turned it forty-five degrees. Over his shoulder he asked, "Does that suit you now, Zeb? I just changed the direction of the river for you." People laughed. Devil Anse stepped back. As for those squiggles – they're the hills and valleys. Them spots are where all our folks live, near as I can make out. See, Charley, here's your place down in the hollow near Blackberry Creek. When I'm done, I want you folks to all come over here and find your places on this here map.

"Talk to your neighbors. As long as these bounty hunters are about, it ain't safe to work the woods or farms alone. Travel together, carry your arms, or keep them handy. Run neighborhood patrols regularly. You can work out the details yourselves. Scoop the hawkshaws up and drop them in the Big Sandy if you have to. But shoot only if you're shot at."

"I ain't a'gonna wait til I'm shot before I shoot back," one yelled. But Devil Anse interrupted.

"Boys, we're starting from way behind in this thing. McCoy's done beat us to the punch. He got New York newspapermen over there, filling their heads with garbage, making us out to be polecats that need killing. He's got warrants, and hawkshaws. That brings me to the second thing we need to do." He walked up to the map and pointed at a few spots that looked more like stars. "These here pointy spots are McCoys or folks who stand with them. Stay away from them. No more night raids or the like. This ain't their makins'. My own son Johnse married a McCoy. We all know the law in these parts don't count for much, but we got to use the little of it what's there. I wrote a letter to Governor Wilson explaining our side in this dispute. We'll see what comes of it. Until I hear back, we're gonna protect our kin and stay out of Kentucky, unless you go armed and in groups." He glared at the room. "Can you boys handle that?" Then he walked over to a bench by the wall, took out a pipe, and sat down, looking for all the world like he was enjoying a picnic.

As it was obvious the meeting was over, the room came to life, buzzing with conversation. The gathering had begun in anger and frustration. Devil Anse had steered it to hope and unified action. Many crowded around the map, locating their properties and determining their plans for patrolling their neighborhoods.

See Bird approached the clan leader who, as was typical for him, was alone, arms crossed, looking both patriarchal and fierce. Seeing the young Choctaw, Devil Anse's face moved not a muscle, but in his eyes, See Bird thought he detected a twinkle of good humor. "That was a good meeting. You gave those boys plenty to chew on."

Devil Anse grunted, removed his pipe and said, "Them boys needed something to do or else they'd be raising Cain, rocking houses up and down the hollers. This'll keep them busy while the government over in Charleston figures out what to do with the government down in Lexington. Oh, they'll do something, all right. Wilson don't really care much for Buckner over in Kentucky. He cain't get reelected here if he looks to be pushed around by a Kentucky bully. And Buckner sure as Satan, cain't get re-elected if he turns the McCoys against him."

"You seem to know a lot about politics," See Bird observed.

Devil Anse emptied his pipe on the floor, sat it carefully beside him on the bench and, hitching his thumbs in his pants pockets said carefully, "Red, just because I live back in the hills don't mean I'm blind or deef to what's going on elsewhere. I make a good living off knowing the timber and mineral industry. Ran'l and me go back a long ways. I think he could forgive a lot – the deaths between us pretty much cancel each other out. We've both lost close kin. But one thing he can never forgive is the success I've had over the years. For some reason, he blames me for it and wants to tear me down, all the while telling himself he's doing it to get even for killing his sons what killed my brother. In a funny way, I feel kinda sorry for the bitter dog he's become. But you tell me now, how are you and Sally getting on?"

"We're doing just fine, thank you for asking. I bought some hogs from over by Upland. I got to pick them up pretty soon. Once we get Sally's Rhode Island Reds tomorrow and the milk cows next week, I do believe we'll be nearly set."

"Good, because I've got a chore I was wondering if you'd take on. I talked to Cap, and even though Jim is dead now, my son's still willing to turn himself in. I think it's a good idea, but with things breaking hard the way they are, I cain't take him to Logan myself, and I don't want him to go alone."

See Bird nodded. Devil Anse continued, "I was hoping you'd be able to see your way free to escort him over to the county seat, Red. It'll be more dangerous now than ever, once we start chasing these hawkshaws down. Levicy has already asked me to invite Sally and Gertrude up for a stay. We'd be proud to have them."

See Bird considered for a moment. He would be glad to do it, but leaving his new family at such a perilous time bothered him greatly. Also, there was no guarantee Sally would go along with the proposal. That gal would have to decide for herself, the way she always did. Finally he spoke, "I'm honored that you asked me," he said. "I've got to clear it with Sally first, and I'll let you know in a day or two. Is that good enough?"

Devil Anse smiled. "When Sally was just a mite of a girl, before we moved up here, the feud had flared up. Her pa never did amount to a hill of beans, wouldn't even let her go to school, and we set that school up only 'bout a half-mile from her house, but her ma was my sister. Sometimes I watch Sally and I see my sister Emmy in her smile or the tilt of her head when she's trying to make her face look mean. Anyhow, one day I showed her how to shoot the 30.06 when I was taking a snooze so that I would be sure that when I woke up it would be in this world and not the next. I had her prop it up on a window sill and told her to let fly if anyone she didn't recognize rode in. She didn't have to hit 'em, just scare them off. I was just dozing off when 'BLAM', she let 'er rip. In the time it took to pop open my eyes, the shotgun was lying on the floor, smoking, and that little thing was peeling herself off the opposite wall. The kick of that gun had nearly broke her shoulder. But she never cried a tear. As I watched, she picked herself up, pushed the hair out of her eyes, the way she's always doing, and retrieved that gun, propping it back on the window ledge. "I was testing it out," she said without looking at me, "I'll do better the next time. You can go back to sleep, Uncle Devil Anse," was what she said and stared out that window again over the top of the shotgun, her eyes all squinty and her lips set. She has her own stubborn way of doing things, and if you hadn't told me you would check it out with her first, I would have figured you for a danged fool." Both men laughed.

Devil Anse placed a hand on See Bird's back and steered him toward the door. "Oh, and by the way, ol' Fletch Ball from over at Ball's gap, swears he put you up with his'n summer before last for a spell and allows how you fixed up a broken down hay wagon for him. Then you headed on south."

"See Right," the younger man exhaled. "He was through here, and he's okay. Thanks, Devil Anse. I can't tell you how much I appreciate your asking about. The older man gazed at See Bird sympathetically and nodded his head, wondering what family feelings moved this young man from the West, a young man from a background so different from his own.

The meeting over, some men were already collecting

their buggies and families and starting their journeys back to their homes in the neighboring hollows. A few, from more distant settlements, were over at the house, still visiting. They would spend the night and start back in the morning. Gertrude was racing about the yard with a cluster of other children, squealing and laughing, oblivious to the grown-ups talking in subdued groups. See Bird looked for Sally and spotted her in a few moments, sitting on a corner of the porch, holding hands and talking quietly with Mary, the young widow of Jim Vance. Sally saw him approaching and flashed him a small, sad smile.

"See Bird, if you don't mind I'm having Mary stay with us for a while 'til she figures out what she's going to do next. I don't want her out in that cabin by herself with all this going on. It ain't safe."

"Absolutely, darlin'." And turning to the young widow he added, "Mary, you stay with us as long as you want to. And if there's anything you need, just ask."

Mary gathered herself up and with pained dignity said, "Thank you, the both of you. I cain't tell you what your kindness means to me. I got some kin on Jim's side over toward Barboursville. Soon's I get things here in order, sell off the land and such, I'll be headed there." She paused, then continued, "You two are so sweet, and Red, I think you done saved Jim's soul. I know he didn't amount to much and done some bad things, but he was sorry and was on his way to set things right when this happened. It don't really matter how you start out your life, now does it? What matters is how you end it." With that she cleared her throat and added, "When you two are ready to head out, just let me know. Now I should say goodbye to Levicy. It'll probably be the last time I ever lay eyes on her," she sighed.

As she disappeared into the house, See Bird told Sally about his conversation with Devil Anse, all but the part about her getting keeled over by the shotgun blast. "In a nutshell," he concluded, "We thought it wise for you to stay here while Cap and me go to Pikeville."

Sally looked directly at See Bird. "Is that right, Bird? Is that what you two decided?" She had begun calling him that when she was upset about something, so her use of the nickname put him on guard.

"Well, not really," he said defensively. "I thought it best to talk it over with you first. But you see it's the only way to go, don't you?"

"In the first place, while that's sugar-sweet of them to offer, and I hope you told them so, I ain't going to do it. Now hold your horses and hear me out. I thought you two men was working up something, but here's the problem as I see it." She took a deep breath and plunged on. "What do you think will happen to our place sitting down there all open to whoever strolls by if there ain't nobody there to protect it. If those scabrous creatures return they're likely to burn it down for spite." Seeing he would need quite a bit more convincing, she added in a softer tone. "Besides that, we got us patrols now, what'll check on us regular-like 'til you return. And Mary'll help with the chores and keep me company."

"But what if, in spite of all that, we do get unwanted company?"

Sally took See Bird by the elbow, guiding him toward Gertrude, who was deeply absorbed floating sticks in the watering trough. "Darling, I never told you, but I'm a fair hand with the shotgun. Devil Anse taught me when I was but a young-un myself. Now that's that and that's all there is to it." See Bird stood speechless, his jaw agape. As if that clinched the argument, Sally turned from him to address her daughter. "Gertrude," Sally scolded, "look at you, soaking wet. My lands."

4

See Bird threw his hand-tooled saddle over the broad back of the chestnut, cinching it snugly and stepping into the stirrup without a word. Cap had arrived near daybreak, and after coffee and two heaping helpings of Sally's flannel-cakes, everyone stepped outside for their goodbyes. Still anxious for the safety of his new family, See Bird had argued with Sally that she should go with Mary and Gertrude up to Devil Anse's place until he would return tomorrow evening.

Sally, though, got in the last word when she swung around from the stove wielding a cast iron skillet. "Bird," she warned in a tone that brooked no opposition, "if you don't stop talking about that right now, I'm gonna mash your head with this here frying pan. I ain't no child and I can take care of myself. Now, that's that, and that's all there is to it!" she said with emphasis, slamming the frying pan down on the stove and setting her back against him. The room seemed overly crowded as the mood turned sour and silent.

See Bird said no more about the subject, nor about anything else. A taciturn man by nature, in his concern and frustration he found himself unable to find the words he needed to convey his loving concern. Now here it was time to say goodbye, both he and Sally were unhappy, yet neither could see a way to close the gap that had opened between them. Cap, mounted also, finally broke the silence. Speaking to Mary he said, "I've got a little money buried under a loose floorboard beneath my bed over at my place. Where I'm going, I won't be needing it for a long time. I want you to have it. It ain't much but it's all I got. I just wish I could've done more to protect Jim. Will you please use it, Mary?"

She started to refuse, hesitated, then nodded, "I will do that, Cap, not because you owe me anything, but just because of my need." She looked up at his face, "but someday I promise I will repay your kindness. Now good luck to the both of you."

See Bird sat uneasily on his mount, not ready to go, but unable to remain. "Ma, lift me up." It was Gertrude. Sally bent and hoisted the child up to See Bird, who sat her on the saddle facing him. "Bye, Pap," she said. Her sad eyes said much more. "I'm gonna miss you awful, so hurry back to me." Her little hands played with the sides of his face while she talked. Then she forced a smile and leaned into a bear-hug, wrapping her arms around his neck.

"You bet I will, you little darlin'. And you obey your ma while I'm gone. Okay?" He felt her nod her head solemnly into his shoulder and ever so carefully he unwrapped her arms and handed her down to Sally. The child passing between them seemed to soften both hearts. To his wife he said, "Well, gal, I've said it all, probably way too much. I just can't stand the idea of anything happening to you." His eyes looked pleadingly at her.

Sally stood, her dark eyes shiny, clutching Gertrude to her bosom, feeling her heart melt for this man who could not tell her how he felt. "I know that, you danged fool. Don't you realize I got the same worrisome feelings for you? Now you go, but hurry home. We'll be here waiting."

See Bird's face was taut, his lips drawn in a line. Touching the brim of his black slouch hat in salute to Mary, he heeled Kiamichi into a canter. Cap followed. The women watched until the riders disappeared into the woods. Gertrude's head was tucked into Sally's breast. "I don't want Pap to go," she complained.

"I know, honey," her mother said softly, "neither do I, but he'll be back tomorrow. Will you help me bake up something special for when he gets home?"

"Yes!" she exclaimed, warming to the idea, "and I know just what Pap likes – a rhubarb pie."

On reaching the shade of the forest, the two men immediately slowed their horses to a fast walk. Their eyes constantly scanned the brush along the sides of the trail and ahead of them as far as they could see. They confined their conversation mainly to the short breaks they took periodically to stretch their legs or to answer nature's call. Cap wore a Colt strapped to his waist. See Bird carried only his knife, but the Winchester rested unstrapped in its sheath over the horse's left shoulder. By mid-morning they crossed a number of trails and tracks, sometimes as wide as a road, at other times so narrow two horses could scarcely ride side-by-side, all of which wound up, over, and around the hills to the various coves and hollows. See Bird remembered how confused he was when he first came to this area. On an overcast day, he got completely turned around, and it was not until he asked directions of a traveler he met along the way, that he got himself straightened out. Today was not such a day, and he had been to Logan several times already, so when the two men stopped alongside a clear brook to eat some of the vittles Sally and Mary had packed for them, See Bird relaxed, releasing much of the morning's anxieties.

Cap bit into a cold meat sandwich and said, "Red, I really appreciate what you're doing and all. It's just that on a day like this, when I think about being locked up for years probably, it makes me consider maybe I should just disappear or take off west or something. But then I think on this lousy feud, and how it will just keep going, and folks dying if I run, so here I am back with you in the woods on my way to prison. I know Pa's heartily disappointed with me. My older brother Johnse married Nancy McCoy. Now she's taken his two kids and left him to move back with her family. Pa was counting on me, and I let him down. Now my life is ruined."

"Cap, you're wrong," See Bird stated with conviction and continued, "I talked with Devil Anse, and I'm telling you he's proud of the way you're manning up. And your life ain't no ways ruined. You got plenty of time to straighten out and make something good out of it.

"Like what, Red? What on earth can I do?"

Red took a final swig from his canteen and, dipping it in the brook to refill, thoughtfully continued, "You can read and write, for one thing. That's more than most of the folks around here can say, more than my Sally can say." He screwed the lid back on and fixed Cap. "So read books, study on things a bit. Lord knows you'll have the time. You've had a run in with the law. Why not study what's put you in the hoosegow so you can keep out of it in the future?"

Cap almost spat out his mouthful of food, erupting in laughter, "Wouldn't that be something, Red? Could you just picture me a lawyer? Don't that just beat all? Where do you come up with ideas like that?"

But See Bird noticed Cap hadn't turned the suggestion down flat on its face. "Cap, you ain't ruined 'til your heart tells you so. And then you still got one more place to turn." He laughed. "Listen to me, sounding like Preacher Anse. It's time we got a move on, don't you think?" Cap swallowed and nodded, and both men soon remounted to continue their journey.

Shortly after they rounded a bend in the trail, from an intersecting trail rode four men in the direction from which See Bird and Cap had just come, missing the two by only a few minutes. The lead rider, weasel-faced and unshaven, spotted the place where Cap and See Bird had recently taken their lunch break. "Someone's been here not long ago, boss," he said. "Looks like more than one. Musta headed down that trail." He pointed. Should we go after them? Might be some money in it for us."

"Nah, they're gone and on horseback." He sounded disappointed. "It'd probably end up a wild goose chase. We'll head on this way. There's a house ahead a piece I want to pay another visit to. I didn't like that boy's attitude what lived there. Besides," he paused and bit off a chaw of tobacco, "it might just be there'll be easier pickins' thataway." He reached into his soiled and threadbare vest and unpinned the tin star, tucking it into a shirt pocket. "C'mon boys," he said and led his men up the trail towards See Bird's farm. "Just stay behind me when we ride in. We'll go in together and then spread out. I don't fancy staring down the barrel of that runt's Winchester again."

Mary, strewing some corn for the newly arrived hens, while Sally and Gertrude were inside the house rolling out dough for a rhubarb pie crust, looked up upon hearing the sighing blow of approaching horses. Four riders emerged from the wooded shadows and advanced at a slow, steady walk. Her heart froze in her chest as she recognized at least two of them, men who had butchered her husband Jim scarcely three days before. Dropping the corn basket where she stood, Mary spun and sprinted for the house. "Sally, get your gun!" she yelled. "Murderers is here!"

The men on horseback sped up, rapidly closing the distance between themselves and the fleeing woman. "Eaf, cut her off," Coburn ordered, and one man sprinted his horse ahead, pulling up between Mary and the porch. Quickly dismounting, he spread his arms, barring her escape. "Now where are you running to?" Coburn asked from the saddle as he reined up. Mary stared in terror. The dawning realization of where he had seen her before lit Coburn's face with a wicked smile as he pointed and wagged a finger at her. "Boys, don't you recognize this little lady? She was the one we ran into in the woods the other day – tried to warn those fellers. Matter of fact one of 'em got clean away. I'm guessing if we ask real politely maybe…" The blast of a shotgun cut him off.

"Mary, get in here!" Sally commanded from the porch. Seeing her chance, Mary dashed up onto the porch and into the house. Sally never lowered the gun, but kept it pointed straight at Coburn. The one he called Eaf lay in the dirt before the house, moaning in pain. The blast had thrown him face down in the grass, his backside a bloody mess, his clothes shredded. "Mister," Sally barked, "you picked the wrong place to ride in on. Now drag that piece of dirt outta here and get off my property or you'll catch the other barrel."

"You can't get all of us, you little witch. You only got one shot left."

"Like I said," Sally repeated, "get off my property or you'll catch the other barrel. This gun's heavy, and I ain't gonna hold it all day. Now move."

Coburn hesitated for just a moment before cursing in frustration, “Suggs, Cob, grab ahold of Eaf and carry him over by that shed.” Coburn then collected the horses and turned to walk away as the other two men struggled with the mangled body. They looked up fearfully at the woman with the gun. “Don’t worry about her, boys. She won’t shoot you in the back. Move it,” Coburn ordered and turned away. The shotgun wavered just a fraction from Sally’s shoulder.

The fearful look on the face of one of the men dissipated as he gazed back at her, replaced by a look of amusement. “Cob, I know her,” he grinned as they lugged the body away. “I know that little whore.”

Sally struggled to keep the shotgun aimed in the general direction of the retreating men until they disappeared behind the shed. Then she backed into the house. “Mary, take this gun and bend your head out that window toward the shed. But don’t show yourself too much. I gotta sit down a minute. Where’s Gertrude?”

“Here I am, Ma,” her little voice answered. She ran and hugged Sally around the legs as her ma collapsed into a chair. “And why did that bad man call you a horse?”

Sally’s eyes gentled as she stroked her daughter’s black, curly hair. “Don’t you worry about it, honey. Those are bad men, but your Pap will be home tomorrow. If fighting starts again, you climb that ladder to the loft and hide way under your bed. You mustn’t come out ‘til I say so. And you mustn’t make a peep.” She cradled the little girl’s head in her hands and looked into her eyes. “Will you promise to do that?” Gertrude nodded. “Okay, then. I’m sorry, darling but it looks like your pap’s pie will have to wait.”

From the window facing the shed, Mary said, “Now would be a good time to reload this thing. Where’s the shells kept?”

Sally's shoulders slumped, "My Lord, what else can go wrong? See Bird just got that thing yesterday. He uses the Winchester but thought after those same men came-a-calling the last time, a shotgun would be handier. The ammo's still out in the shed in a poke under the window. I was going to bring it in this morning but forgot." Her voice sounded plaintive. "Make it count, Mary. That one shot is all we got."

Behind the shed, the three remaining men were taking stock of their situation. "Eaf's pretty well shot up," Cob said. Lost so much blood he might not make it. Really, we ought to get him to a doctor."

Coburn thought a moment. "No, I don't think so," he said. "He wouldn't make it anyhow. And that one woman saw us the other day and you could bet your bottom dollar she would like nothing better than to make trouble for me. I can't let her do that. Besides that, I think these gals are here by theyselves. I don't see no men about. I do believe the three of us can handle two little women. Leastways they can't get the drop on us again. Damn, I wish that little one hadn't shot up Eaf. Still, if he dies, that's one less man to split the money up with."

"Boss, I'm sure I know her," Suggs chimed in. "For sure, she's a little whore who works down at Frog Island."

Coburn said nothing for a minute, his brow wrinkled in unaccustomed thought and his eyes unfocused. "So that's their game," he snapped. "This is a cathouse for them hillbillies. It explains a lot, and why there ain't no menfolk about right now. Well, now that I see what's going on here, we might as well sit back and wait until dark while I work us out a plan." He smiled inwardly as he visualized how he was going to make those two women pay for what they did to Eaf.

5

Harmon Phillips knew he and his 'posse' were deep in West Virginia illegally, but the lure of all the bounty money Kentucky was offering for Hatfields dead or alive made the risk worth it. The reward for Devil Anse himself was a magnet drawing men from all over the country. Five hundred bucks. A man could work more than a year and not see money like that. Granted, Devil Anse was not likely to come strolling down this road, but his scouts had reported that other men, undoubtedly Hatfields or their sympathizers, had been recently using these same trails. And there were bounties on many heads.

Near a ford over a tributary of the Tug Fork, he deployed his posse of eighteen men in the surrounding brush and woods. Anyone crossing the stream would be exposed to a deadly crossfire. As he was checking on his men's concealment a rider thundered into the small clearing and yanked his horse to a halt. "Harmon," he warned excitedly, "they's a band of riders headed this way, maybe half-a-dozen – armed."

"Hide your horse and take cover," he ordered. "Okay, men," he whispered loudly, "get ready, and don't shoot 'til I say so." Hearing the rattle of horses coming down the trail from behind him, he stood, momentarily confused, and then decided he would be better off hidden too. Immediately after he dashed into cover, a group of seven riders descended the trail behind the ambush site toward the stream. Before they could cross, however, the six riders previously spotted, emerged from the cloak of the woods on the far side of the stream.

The two groups drew up on opposite banks and hailed each other. "Elias," the leader of the horsemen on the far side called, "it's me, Bill Dempsey. Sheriff Miller over in Logan heard about the troubles and sent some men to help calm things down."

"That's right good of him, Bill," Elias responded, "'cause we sure can use all the help we can get. Come on over." He waved Dempsey across and backed his horse as the men on the far side started down into the water.

Suddenly a voice cried from the woods, "Open fire, boys. Let 'em have it." Instantly, the hollow erupted with a cacophony of gunfire. Horses reared and riders tumbled and dove to the ground. A few unholstered their pistols and returned fire, their terrified horses making it impossible to take aim, even if their riders could see who was shooting at them from the foliage.

Bill Dempsey, just emerging from the water, saw the futility of resistance and waved his arms, all the while yelling, "Cease fire! Cease fire!" A sudden burning pain in his leg made it impossible to remain mounted, and he slid to the ground. All around him men were dropping their guns and raising their hands into the air, staring into the underbrush.

"Okay, men, cease fire," Phillips ordered. The smell of gun smoke hung heavy in the damp air as men pointing pistols emerged from behind what seemed like every tree. "Kneel down!" he yelled. When a couple men hesitated for a second, he fired his pistol just over their heads. "I said kneel down once, and I ain't gonna tell you again."

"I cain't kneel," Dempsey said. "I been shot."

"Is that right?" Phillips mocked and strutted over to where the wounded man lay. "And who might you be?"

"Name's Bill Dempsey. I'm the deputy sheriff from over at Logan. I need a doctor."

"Deputy sheriff, eh? Looks to me like you're just another stinking Hatfield." He stood over the wounded man, and Dempsey knew he was staring into the eyes of death. "Might be there's money on your head, too." He cocked his pistol and calmly shot the wounded man between the eyes. "Take this bag of guts and shove it in the brush someplace. I had to shoot him when he tried to escape. You got that?" he said as he rounded on the rest of the men. "Collect the guns, and koffle the prisoners with rope. I guess we're going to have us a pretty pay day when we haul this crew into Pikeville. Now get moving."

"Harmon," his second in command said, once they were mounted and heading back up the trail west, "we sure enough bagged a bunch, but three of them turned and ran back up this trail and got clean away."

"Three, huh. That's too bad. Still, I don't imagine three cowards can do us much harm. Tell the men to keep their eyes open, just the same. We can't take any chances with our valuable freight." Each prisoner was lashed to his saddle with his hands tied behind his back. Several ropes knotted together comprised the koffle, a term originating with the African slave trade and adapted now to a different use. A continuous rope noosed around each prisoner's neck and looped around his hands, tied behind his back. Should one man fall from his horse, intentionally or otherwise, the action would cause a chain reaction of tightening nooses around the necks of the other prisoners. Nine sullen and beaten men, thus noosed together, with the rope tied to the saddle of a guard riding directly ahead of the string, were trailed by two more men acting as the rear guard. The rest of the posse rode ahead in a jostling, joking mass. Things for them had gone well, indeed, much better than some had feared. These mountaineers hadn't turned out to be nearly as fearsome as they were made out.

See Bird halted in the trail and gestured for Cap to do the same. He leaned forward, straining to listen. "I don't hear it now, but I believe I heard gunfire popping up ahead, I'd guess a mile or more. Hard to tell in these woods. But it was there, and enough of it for me to be pretty sure it was no hunter." He thought a moment and then continued. "If we go forward, we may ride into something we might regret. We could turn around, but we already been there. Might be we could work our way around, but I'm not real familiar with the byways in these parts. What do you think, Cap?"

"Red, I'll take your word on the gunfire. But I gotta tell you, I been raised in these woods and I didn't hear a thing. Seems to me that if you're right, now we been warned. If we just go on real cautious, we can deal with what's up ahead when we get there." He hesitated, now indecisive, "But maybe we should go back to the farm and try tomorrow. I don't…"

The conversation was interrupted by the drumming of horse hooves pounding up the trail. Quickly, the two men walked their mounts off the road and waited, guns drawn, staring in the direction they were headed. From around a corner about a hundred yards away and below them appeared three riders. From the sound and looks of their horses, the men had been riding them hard. The horses puffed to a walk as they started up the incline.

"Them's our boys," Cap whispered. "I'd know Shelby Hatfield anywhere. And the two behind him are Virgil Cline and Henry Martin. Something surely has them spooked." He stepped his horse out onto the trail and hailed the approaching riders.

Shelby reined up so hard his horse nearly dumped him on the road. The other two fumbled as if looking for their guns. "Hold it men. Back off. It's me, Cap Hatfield and Red Carpenter."

"Is that really you, Cap? By God, it is. Men, hold up a minute. Put your guns away."

"You boys like to run your horses into the ground," See Bird commented. "What happened down the trail? We thought we heard gunfire back a bit."

"Well, you most surely did, old son," Henry Martin spoke up excitedly. "We was ambushed down by Blackberry Creek. We had just ran into a posse coming from Logan led by Bill Dempsey when all hell broke loose. I saw him hit the ground and figured that place was too hot for me."

"Why did this posse from Logan shoot at you men?"

"Dang it, Cap, if you ain't thick headed as a brick," Cline spat in frustration. "It warn't them what shot at us. Someone was waiting in the woods and just started in a shooting. They seemed to be everywhere, maybe hundreds."

The one called Shelby spoke up softly but firmly, "There warn't no 'hundreds.' I been thinking on it while we rode. It was a good ambush, well set. The bushwhackers sprang it just right, but maybe a minute too soon." Cline looked at him as if to question his conclusion. "We got away, didn't we?" Shelby continued. "Another few yards and they'd have bagged us all. Then there'd be no one to tell the tale. I would guess there was maybe a couple dozen men – at the most."

See Bird liked this man Shelby. Of the three, he seemed the most composed. He thought about the odds for a moment, then spoke. "We got to decide what to do now, 'cause them hombres will come a calling in about ten – fifteen minutes tops. No doubt they're planning on taking the men back to Pikeville. If they do so, you can lay money on it that this country will become a regular hunting grounds, worse than it already is, for them bounty hunters. We got to stop them."

"But what can we do, Red, with only the five of us against that mob?"

"Let's walk our horses back up the trail a ways. I got an idea that maybe we can ambush the ambushers. Now wouldn't that be fun, getting' in some licks for a change 'stead of always being on the receiving end?" The men grunted their approval, and their eyes flickered with nascent hope. As See Bird turned back up the road he smiled – and wondered to himself what in fact five men could do against so many.

The summer sun was well past its meridian when the first echoes of lowered voices and the harder drumming of hooves warned See Bird and his small band of men of the approaching Kentucky posse. Well concealed, he and Shelby squatted in the heavy branches of a thick oak that straddled the trail on a switchback which concealed the rear of the column from its head. This was to be up-close-and-personal knife work. The timing must be perfect, their drops must be on target, and it was essential they dispose of the two rear guards before they could raise an alarm, in silence. See Bird and Shelby doubled back and scouted the troop to ascertain their order of march, then took a short cut back to clarify the plan with Cap and the others. Everyone had a vital role to play, but disaster loomed before them if See Bird or Shelby were to fail.

Following the jingling, chatting, slow moving mob rode the man leading the nine man prisoner koffle. After the last captive were the two rear guards, the final rider leading Bill Dempsey's horse with all the captives' hardware in saddle bags.

Shelby watched See Bird for the hand signal. When he lowered his arm they both dropped simultaneously. Because of the guards' slightly different spacing, See Bird fell a moment sooner, dropping onto the rump of the horse, immediately behind the saddle. The other guard saw what was happening but before he could warn anyone Shelby had plunged onto his back, knocking them both from the horse. After only a momentary struggle Shelby's man lay still, and as he looked up See Bird was sliding into his man's vacant saddle, cleaning his blade on the saddle blanket. "Mount up. We're not done yet." Shelby leaped astride his mount.

Their attack occurred so suddenly and silently that the last captive had not even noticed the disturbance behind him. They would have only a couple minutes until the front of the column reached the three men See Bird had hidden. See Bird and Shelby had to work fast. Riding up alongside the last prisoner, See Bird reached over and slashed the rope off his wrists. Seeing what was afoot, the man lifted the noose from his neck and as he dropped behind, following See Bird's hand gesture, Shelby handed him a pistol. The freed man's visage was grim. A minute ago he was humiliated and ashamed. Now unexpectedly he was granted a chance at redemption. He would succeed or die trying.

See Bird and Shelby quickly worked their way up the line. His original intention was to free as many captives as possible and then to fade away. But the terrain was so favorable to an ambush he decided to roll the dice and try to turn the table on the kidnappers. Cap,

Henry, and Virgil were in place up ahead, concealed on an embankment formed by an unfinished railway cut. They had dragged a large dead tree across the road to block it, but were not to start any gunplay until and unless they heard it coming from the rear of the column. If they heard nothing they were to fade into the shadows and head back to See Bird's farm in Warm Hollow.

The noise of the approaching column could now be heard distinctly. It would be only a matter of moments before the lead elements rounded this end of the switchback and spotted the tree barring their path. At that point, if they heard nothing the concealed men would have to disengage or risk joining the long line of prisoners. Cap wondered if something had gone wrong. It seemed to him that something always did, and it left a bitter taste in his mouth. He raised his arm to back the other two off as the lead riders rounded the bend. Nothing seemed out of the ordinary. The men rode at their ease. But Cap's arm froze in midair as he heard the distant popping of what had to be small arms fire. The lead riders were disturbed but at first appeared confused as to what was causing the disruption behind them. Almost immediately the sound of gunfire rose to a crescendo and the pressure from the rear of the column began forcing the horses in the front into a state of panic, wanting to flee the noise and chaos while their riders fought to have them face the onrushing column. The narrow trail, scarcely wide enough at that point to allow two horses side-by-side, compounded the problem. The question of whether to flee or stand was settled for them by the rear of the column exerting an irresistible force. Like a dam bursting, as if everyone had made up their minds at the same time, the posse spun their mounts and spurred forward on the run.

"Wait," Cap said. "Wait – Now! Let 'em have it." The three men on the cut-bank opened up with all the firepower they had as See Bird led his band of enraged mountaineers, slashing and smashing with rifles and gun butts, their way through the disorganized mob, not giving them a moment's time to regroup or even to figure out what happened. One posse member turned his horse sideways, blocking See Bird's progress, trying to face the direction of the action. Before he could complete the maneuver, however, See Bird brought up the stock of the Winchester and cracked the side of his head, tumbling him from the saddle. The mountaineers followed his lead, cutting a swath through the posse, unseating and disarming its men, shouting and shooting, mostly into the air, adding now one, now another to the growing mass of stunned, surrendering men.

A few of the Kentucky posse at the fore dismounted and tried at first to drag the blocking tree aside, but coming quickly under fire from unseen assailants on the cut-bank above them, they decided it was too dangerous in the open and settled down in whatever cover they could find beneath the big tree. A pair of riders tried to provide supporting fire for the men working on the tree, but their pitching and rearing horses rendered their attempts completely ineffective.

The gunfire from the rear became more sporadic and then ceased altogether as the Kentucky posse members were themselves taken captive and quickly disarmed. See Bird and Shelby burst through the head of the column, Kiamichi prancing in his excitement. Used to crowds and noise, he was not panicked in the least. The quarter horse remembered his training and trusted his rider implicitly. See Bird saw the two mounted men before the downed tree, focused on the gunfire raining from above, were the only ones now returning fire.

He quickly surveyed the scene and ordered Shelby to round up the captives. See Bird shoved his Winchester back in its sheath and swung his mount around. Shelby admired the distinctive way See Bird rode, erect, reins loose in his hands, not a hint of a slouch. His horse and he seemed to be reading each other's minds. As Kiamichi leaped forward, See Bird lifted a coil of rope from beside the saddle and, with the reins in his teeth, spun out his lariat in an ever-widening circle over his head.

In spite of the gunfire still aimed in their general direction from the two men sitting their horses directly below them, Cap could not resist peering through the leaves to observe what was happening farther down the trail. Occasionally he, Virgil, and Henry would throw a shot of return fire. The two horsemen sitting side-by-side, firing up into the underbrush, never saw the noose fly out of See Bird's hand and dally directly over their heads, but they felt it snugly settle over them both. Yanking hard, See Bird tightened the noose, pinning the men's arms to their sides, and tying off the rope to the saddle horn. On his command, Kiamichi dug in his hooves, stopped, and started backing quickly, yanking both men out of their saddles and leaving them stunned on the ground. As they tried to regain their feet, See Bird's mount would back a few more paces, sending them tumbling back onto the ground. See Bird smiled from the saddle and cradled his rifle as another recently freed West Virginian rode up and jumped to the ground to collect the roped men's fallen weapons. The last two posse members hiding in the cover of the downed tree saw that somehow their fortunes had been reversed and crawled out, tossing their guns into the road before them and raising their hands. With their surrender, all resistance ceased and a cry of jubilation and victory rolled up and down the trail, just as the famed Rebel Yell of a bygone era had similarly resounded over so many battlefields.

Later on, in the retelling of 'The Battle of the Cut Bank,' as it became known, many of the participants would not recognize themselves: They had grown larger than life. A few men, it was said, had routed a force ten times its size using only knives and a rebel yell. Cap and his small band, it was said, had repelled multiple charges up the cut bank, exhausting their ammo and having to resort to throwing rocks and logs down on their attackers. And the largest legend grew around See Bird, who in the telling was everywhere at once, who feathered into the enemy ranks and cut through them like a hot knife through butter, who became, in the retelling both the commanding general and an avenging angel .

But on the ground after the battle, he was more concerned about the immediate situation. Miraculously, not one of the West Virginians was wounded. The same, however, could not be said of the Kentucky posse. Two had fallen and would not rise again. Three more had wounds, none of them life-threatening. These were bound up the best way they could while See Bird and Cap held a conference to determine what was to be done with the sixteen prisoners, several of whom needed medical attention.

"Red, if that weren't the darndest thing," Cap said with a grin that lit up the young man's face. "It is gonna be worth it for me to surrender just so's we could roust up all these hawkshaws. But what are we gonna do with 'em all?"

See Bird looked at the young man sitting before him. He certainly had some of his father's temper and courage, yet his spontaneous, outgoing nature must have been inherited from his mother. He hoped Cap could find a way to blend the best of both. It seemed a tragedy to See Bird that because of one thoughtless night of violence, Cap was destined to spend much of his life in prison. What, he wondered, would the experience do to such a personality? He shook his head and brought his thoughts back to the question he had been asked.

"Well, Cap, as I see it, really nothing much has changed except now we got us a lot more company. If we get a move on, we should be able to herd this bunch over to Logan and turn them in to the law by nightfall. Kidnapping is against the law most everywhere, I think, including West Virginia. They'll deal with them there, we'll be rid of them, and then you and me will do whatever we got to do."

"I guess you're right, Red," he replied in a subdued voice, but unable to sustain it he added with gusto, "but I do believe I will remember this day for the rest of my life – Whoo-ey!" He slapped his leg and they rose together.

See Bird admired the way Shelby had taken it upon himself to arrange the prisoners, two to a horse, facing each other, arms lashed around each other. The picture it presented to the mountaineers who held them captive became the subject of unending hoots of derision and laughter.

"Now you boys just behave yourselves up there, you hear? There'll be no sparkin' in the saddles!" someone shouted. A few of the bound men cursed with a fury, but that only brought down upon them more hilariously profane attention. They soon subsided into a sullen and demoralized silence.

"All right then, men. Let's turn this mob around and ride them in to Logan. I don't want to nursemaid these scum buckets any longer than I have to, so we'll ride 'til we get there. If nature calls, take care of your business and then catch up. If any of the prisoners feel such a necessity," See Bird paused for effect, then continued, "well now I don't reckon snakes got that kind of problem, do they? So don't worry about it. They can hold it or go in the saddle. I'm sure his saddle-mate will appreciate it and forgive him in Christian charity." The woods echoed with shouts of emphatic agreement. See Bird and Cap took their place at the head of the column. Looking back over his shoulder, See Bird waved forward and shouted, "Head 'em out!" as though he were setting a cattle drive into motion.

The cavalcade thus proceeded amid taunts and jests, back toward the east, in the direction of Logan. As they neared Blackberry Creek, Shelby joined See Bird and Cap at the head and filled them in on how it was that he and his men were captured in the first place. See Bird brought the group to a halt just short of the creek and ordered that Phillips be unbound and brought forward. "Is it true," See Bird asked, "what this gent told me, that right over there in that brush is the body of a real lawman?" Phillips saying nothing, just dropped his eyes. "And is he telling me the truth when he says you shot that wounded man down like a dog?" Again Phillips said not a word, avoiding See Bird's eyes. "I guess it is true then. Listen close, mister." See Bird leaned forward in the saddle, "I'm going to give you a chance to do something right. It don't make up for what you done here, but with the Lord as my witness, you're going to do it proper or you shall die where you stand. You hear me?" He sat back slowly. "Now you go and bring him back over here. Then you go get a slicker and wrap up the body. Then you, all by yourself, lift him up and tie him across his horse so's he can be taken home and given a Christian burial. Shelby, will you be so kind as to accompany Mr. Phillips here, just to make sure he don't get some crazy notion in his head. If he does, please settle his hash for him. We can plant him right here if we have to."

"Be glad to, Red." The lanky mountaineer dismounted and unholstered the big Colt. All the bravado, all the false courage Harmon Phillips had displayed up to this point evaporated in the face of the barrel of the Colt. With considerable difficulty he nonetheless eventually succeeded in tying the body of the murdered lawman to his horse. Then, shaking from exertion and wiping his brow from the sweat of his labor, he moved toward his horse. "Not so fast there," See Bird's call stopped him short. "I want you to think about what it feels like to ride like that – tied across the back of a horse. I want you to think about that dead man and his family all the way into Logan. Boys, take this man and tie him across his saddle like a corpse. I sure do hope he lives all the way into town."

"Now just a minute," Phillips protested. "I did what you said. This ain't human."

See Bird's voice took on the hardness of tempered steel. "Boys, tie him tight."

It was a somber sight that greeted the people of the small town of Logan, West Virginia, that evening just after sunset. The last of the sun's rays were lingering on the peak of Rattlesnake Mountain as the group of over two dozen mounted men rode into the village nestled on the hillsides above the banks of the Guyandotte and made their way to the sheriff's office. The sight of so many men lashed face to face, and the two bodies, one in a sheet, the other obviously miserable but very much alive, guaranteed that a sizable crowd would follow them to find out what was going on.

It did not take long for word to spread that the Hatfields had fought it out with troop of hawkshaws sent by the McCoys, and that these same hawkshaws killed their deputy sheriff, Bill Dempsey. As the word spread, the mood of the crowd turned from celebratory to surly.

See Bird met the sheriff on the jailhouse steps. The two men shook hands perfunctorily. "Sheriff, it appears," he began, "we brought you a bit of a headache and a heartache. That dead man strapped to his horse is Bill Dempsey, your deputy. He was killed by the other man strapped to his horse." Phillips squirmed and mumbled in his fury and discomfort. See Bird turned back to the sheriff. You can do with him whatever you want. I'm glad to be rid of him. We let him ride all the way in like that, resting easy across the saddle and from the tone of his voice he's a mite ungrateful." The sheriff smiled grimly. "Shelby," See Bird turned to the man standing next to him, "would you stuff the rag a bit snugger in his mouth? I don't take much to a cussin' man."

"I'd be glad to, Red." He turned and walked away. Phillips stopped making noise. Bill Dempsey's friends carefully removed his body and carried it away.

"The headache I referred to is that I brought you a wagonload of customers. Those bound men are Kentucky bounty hunters, kidnappers and murderers. They're all yours now. "

"Well, Red, I do believe I can handle them just fine."

"Yes, sir, I'm sure you can. But there's more to it than that. Some of my men here have warrants out for their arrests in Kentucky. We've hashed it out and they would be willing to have their day in court if they could be guaranteed safe passage to Pikeville. There's so many hawkshaws crawling these hills most of the men rightly fear was they to surrender to one of 'em, they'd not live to reach the Pikeville jail. If you was to give them an armed escort, I do believe we could settle things down a mite without the governor calling up the militia." He paused, looking at the eight West Virginians huddled behind him. Grim men all, they nodded agreement. "Most of these boys are hard working men who felt pushed too hard. They got families and children to consider. Long as this continues, there ain't none of them safe. And they know it."

The sheriff rubbed the stubble on his chin and said, "Young man, you've done right, and though I feel terrible for Bill and his widow, I'm glad you did for him what you did. The jail's got but three cells. I'm not worried about space for them polecats." He nodded as his deputies led the bounty hunters into the jail. "We will pack them in." He smiled and said, "It appears they're used to riding close to each other. It's you men, I'm concerned about." He spoke directly to the mountaineers. "If it was up to me, I'd plumb let you go free for what you did today. But it ain't. So I'm gonna ask you for your word of honor that until such a time as I can notify authorities in Pikeville of your presence and intentions and receive their reply, you men will confine yourself to the city of Logan and present yourself to me at such time as I call for. Mrs. Taylor runs a boarding house around the corner and down a block. Can't miss it. She can board eight easily, 'specially if some of you'll share a room. Consider the cost of food and boarding while you're in my jurisdiction taken care of by the city of Logan. It ain't much, but it's the best I can do. What do you say?"

See Bird surveyed the men. While none of them wanted to go to jail in Pikeville, they all realized what was at stake. Cap spoke for them. He extended his right hand and said, "Sheriff Miller, we done wrong and know we gotta pay for it. But we ain't gonna do wrong by you, are we boys?" The men shuffled their feet, clearly wanting to be somewhere, anywhere else. One by one they made eye contact with Cap and nodded their pledge.

"Red Carpenter," the sheriff turned his attention back to See Bird as the other men drifted away in the direction of the boarding house. "I don't reckon I ever heard the name before, but I do expect I'll hear it again. You've done not just this town, but the whole state a favor. My headache will be over in a day or two. But you know, don't you that it's possible some of these boys are gonna get their necks stretched for killing that McCoy girl. How're the folks in your neck of the woods going to like that? Think they'll try to bust them out?"

See Bird shrugged. "Free men have the right to change their minds. Matter of fact, only free men can act on that right. And mountaineers are the freest men I know, so I can't tell you what these men or other men might do in the future. But this is what they decided today. What happens next is up to you, them, and these two states. Now if you'll excuse me, I'm pretty well done in and think I'll head on down to the livery. I noticed on the way in, it felt like my horse was missing a step – feels like a loose nail. Think I'll pay a visit to the blacksmith. Maybe he'll let me throw down there. G'night, sheriff." He touched the brim of his hat in salute and headed down the street. *Mighty fine night*, he thought. *The sheriff was right: With that Kentucky crew under lock and key, this corner of West Virginia should be a much safer place.* The thought of Sally and

Gertrude safely resting at home should have brought a sense of peace to him. Still, for some indefinable reason he felt uneasy. *I probably just feel guilty about leaving them the way I did,* he thought. *Yes sir*, he decided, *I think I'll get an early start back in the morning.*

The livery man was kind enough to let him throw down in a corner on a fresh pile of clean straw. See Bird struggled to gain some rest by focusing on the thought of getting home and sleeping in the bed he built, beside the woman he loved. But sleep was hard a'coming.

6

The hot afternoon wore on with Sally and Mary taking turns keeping watch out the window in the direction of the shed, behind which the four men had disappeared. Tedium soon replaced tension. Even Gertrude, instructed to remain in her bedroom loft for her own safety, began whining after about ten minutes to come down. "It's too hot up here, Ma," she complained at the top of the ladder.

Sally sighed. She knew it wasn't true. It may have been a bit uncomfortable, but See Bird built the loft with a lovely window facing south. Directly below it was the section of porch that curled around the house and ran the length of its west side. On the opposite end of the house was a matching window but with no porch beneath. Both windows were open providing a gentle cross-draft that kept the house from overheating. Below Gertrude's loft was Sally's and See Bird's bedroom with two wonderful windows facing the south and east. Now they, like most of the rest of the windows, were shuttered from the inside for protection. The rest of the structure was open space. To the east of the bedroom was a living area with a stone fireplace. Sally would have preferred a proper parlor, but See Bird had built it this way because, he said, it reminded him of the West, of the open ranch houses where he had spent so much time before coming east. The north half of the downstairs was wide open living, cooking, and eating space, dominated by Sally's kitchen.

The big oval wood-burning stove stood in the place of honor, slightly off-center of the north wall. To its left were open cupboards and a counter for food preparation. Skillets and other cookware hung handily from hooks on a rafter overhead. To the right of the stove was a sink, complete with a hand pump to relieve her from the chore of fetching water. But the crowning glory, the thing Sally was most proud of was the 'indoor outhouse,' as she called it. Very few people in these parts had one, though it was becoming more common in the big cities like Huntington and Charleston. On the northeast corner of the house was the only other door besides the one opening to the porch on the west side. But it did not lead outside. Instead, it opened to a small room that did, in fact, resemble nothing so much as an outhouse. There was the common bench with the hole cut into it, but appearance was the only similarity. Beside the seater-hole was a bucket of water. When finished, the user would dump the water down the hole and flush out the waste, carrying it via a pipe to a 'dry well' See Bird had constructed about thirty feet from the house. The entire contraption worked wonderfully well, and Sally, who could remember running from the home of her youth to the outhouse in the cold of winter or the dead of night, appreciated that little lean-to more than just about anything See Bird had built. *Today especially*, she thought grimly, *with four murderers hiding behind the shed, she appreciated the convenience of indoor water more than ever.*

The long afternoon wore on, each minute seeming like an hour as the two women waited – for what, they were unsure. *Would they be rushed by their assailants and them with only one shot left? Would the men behind the shed wait until dark, when the women were tired and perhaps let their guards down? Or maybe,* they thought optimistically, *the men would just give up and slip away under the cover of darkness.* Somehow, though, no matter how much she wished it or said it, she just didn't believe they would take that route.

As for relief, both women knew that a neighborhood Hatfield patrol might come by at anytime. And See Bird was certain to return tomorrow some time. But did they want their kin to be endangered by men lying in wait? And the image of See Bird riding in completely unaware of the danger, only to be cut down by a fusillade of lead held an unspeakable terror for Sally. With nothing to dwell on but the danger they all were in, her fear for See Bird finally roused her to action even as the evening shadows were beginning their slow march across the hollow.

"We've got to get that ammo out of the shed, Mary," she said. "All those men have to do is walk in here, and there's no way we can stop them."

"Maybe we can't, but they don't know we only got one shot. What do you think's been holding them off all day?" Mary answered, sensing that Sally had some dangerous idea in the works. "And besides that, just in case you hadn't noticed, they're still camped right behind that same shed, that is, if they ain't lit out."

"Well, that's one thing I can check directly." Sally stood and headed towards the door.

"Where you going, gal?"

Sally opened the door and stepped onto the porch. "Just to get a breath of air."

A splinter of wood from the door frame flew by her face an instant before she heard the report of the gun. Ducking back inside and slamming the door, she exhaled, "Well, that's enough fresh air for a while. And you can rest assured them scalping butchers are still watching the house."

"Sally, are you plumb crazy? Trying to get yourself killed?" Mary scolded.

"No, ma'am, I sure ain't. I figured that from behind the shed, if that's where they are, it's too far a distance to get off an accurate pistol shot. Still," she reflected, "that was close enough. And we know now they're still over there. C'mere and listen up. I got a plan. If it works, we'll be sitting pretty."

Mary cocked her head. Although doubtful, the long wait was exhausting her as well. "Go ahead, Sal. I'll listen from over here."

Sally took a deep breath and plunged in. "Mary, we cain't just sit here waiting for them people to shoot whoever walks up, or for them to come a-kickin' the door in themselves. They're watching this door. I could climb out the bedroom window and sneak along the back side of the house. If I can get behind the garden fence that my man built to keep the varmints out of my herbs and vegetables without being seen, I'd only have a few yards to the shed door. Once inside, I'd grab the box of shells and hightail it out the way I come in. If it works out, I'll be back in five minutes."

"And if it don't?"

"If it don't, Mary, at least I will have tried. You'll still be here with the shotgun." Her voice wavered a little. "God bless you for a friend, Mary. Cover me, and take care of the little one upstairs."

"Please don't do this, Sally. We can think of something else. There's got to be another way."

"If you can think of one, please let me know. But make it soon 'cause I ain't gonna wait until dark wraps us up. Right now I'm gonna change out of this blousy dress and put on one of See Bird's jeans and a shirt. I sure cain't do any sneaking around in this frilly thing. I'll be back in a minute. You think on things." Sally returned from the bedroom wearing an extra pair of See Bird's blue jeans, rolled up several times from the bottom and one of his linen long sleeved shirts, buttoned at the wrists so that the sleeves wouldn't swallow her hands. She walked over to the kitchen counter with what she hoped was an air of confidence and started paring an apple. "Gertrude, honey, would you come down here for a minute? I want to talk to you."

"Sure, Ma." The eager little feet scurried down the ladder.

"Here, baby, have an apple slice." Gertrude's chubby hands reached out for the fruit. "And I have something to tell you." She pared another slice for herself. "I'm going outside for a few minutes, and I want to be sure you understand the rules. Until I get back in the house you must stay upstairs. And if the bad men get inside what will you do?"

"Hide way under my bed and be very quiet." She raised a finger to her lips.

"Wonderful, and obey every word Aunt Mary says."

The little girl looked at the other woman, who smiled at her. "I promise. But you look funny in daddy's clothes." She giggled.

"I'll tell you what I'm gonna do, you rascal. Tomorrow, after your Pap gets home, you and me will go on a chicken egg hunt. How does that sound?"

Gertrude's dark eyes widened. She patted her hands together. "Oh, fun."

"All right then, that's that and that's all there is to it." Sally handed the last slice of apple to Mary.

Mary took the slice and stared at it lying in her palm. "I don't know how you can eat at a time like this,

Sally. But if you're ready, so am I. I cain't think of any other plan that don't involve us or someone we love likely dying. I tried, but my Jimmy's still dead, and I'd give anything for the chance to take his place. Maybe you'll be luckier than me. Maybe none of us'll die." She picked up the shotgun and moved to the window. "I'll be covering you." Sally stood for a second staring at her friend's back, then walked up from behind and embraced her. Mary kept facing out the window. *So this is what love looks like,* Sally thought and turned for the bedroom. In a few seconds she rolled out of the window and dropped to the ground. Inside, Gertrude scampered up the ladder back to her loft.

Sally lay on her back for a moment, just catching her breath and working up her courage. Then she rolled onto her stomach and pushed herself up into a low crouch. Thank heavens she had changed clothes. The denim just brushed the rose bushes See Bird had planted for her along the house. Her long dress would have gotten hopelessly entangled in the thorns. Once beside the lean-to she sat for another few seconds, listening to her heart pound. The easy part was over. Sally knew that once she stepped out from behind this wall she would be completely exposed for a few yards until she reached the cover of the short fence See Bird had constructed to keep the rabbits and such out of her herb and vegetable garden.

Her courage wavered. Her imagination conjured up the picture of a gun aimed directly at where she would step, just waiting for her to show herself. She bit her lip, rolled onto her stomach and crawled quickly across the open ground. As soon as she reached the relative safety of the fence, she exhaled forcefully, realizing she had been holding her breath. She gathered her wits and forced herself to breathe normally. It was quieter and helped calm her screaming nerves.

What a fool I am, she thought. *When I was in the house this seemed like the only reasonable plan. But I feel like I'm about to drown in my fears. I am so afraid that I'll just stand up and run screaming back to the house. Please, God,* she prayed, *I know we don't talk much, and that's my fault, I know, but I need a mountain of help right now. You're all I got left to hope on, so don't let my feet stumble between here and that shed over there. That's it. Thanks and maybe I'll be seeing you real soon.* Perhaps it was expressing the simple cry of her heart that calmed her, or maybe there was some supernatural intervention, but whatever the source, Sally felt a calm certainty that things would be all right. A peace settled over her she had not known before.

At the kitchen window, Mary rested the barrel of the shotgun on the window ledge, and kept her eyes glued to the door of the shed. Where was Sally? Was she lying out there hurt someplace? Had somebody grabbed her? In the time it took to blink her eyes she saw a small hunched-over figure dash out from behind the garden fence and disappear into the shadows of the shed. Elated, she had to control herself from cheering. *That could only be Sally*, she thought. *She's made it. She's half-way home, now*. "Grab the ammo and get out. I've got you from here," she muttered, settling down, anticipating every second seeing that same small figure dash back behind that garden fence.

Sally leaned against the inside of the shed door, panting and inhaling the not unpleasant odors of axle grease, oil, and leather that all reminded her of See Bird, her eyes adjusting to the play of shadows in the darkened room. But she had no time to waste. If she had ever thought of jumping from the frying pan into the fire, then this certainly was it. Keenly aware there was only one thin board separating her from the men trying their best to kill her, she moved as silently as possible along one wall towards the only window in the small building. She had placed the gunny sack containing the box of shotgun shells on the floor directly under that window. But now there was nothing there. Not believing her eyes, she knelt down and felt along the floor, growing more frantic by the moment.

"Is this what you're looking for?" Her heart froze in her chest as she heard the metallic click of a gun hammer being cocked. From the shadows emerged the one called Suggs, wearing his familiar blank grin, with a pistol pointed in her direction. "Coburn sent me in here to try to find something useful. And looky here, what I found," he hissed. "Get over here now," he ordered. Sally rose and slowly approached Suggs. "Well, I never," he said. "What have I got me here, all dressed up like a little man?" His eyes searched her obscenely. "But I know for certain that you ain't, don't I?" Sally refused to be cowed. Her eyes flashed defiance, though she wanted to cringe in terror. "I met you when you was working the docks once, down on Frog Island. You probably don't recall, but I can't forget." The gun waved back and forth like a pointer. "You wouldn't take my two-bits. That made me angry. Why wouldn't you take my money? It was as good as anybody's."

Disgust filled Sally, but she realized this man was serious. He honestly wanted to know why she rejected him. "Because you made me sick," she said defiantly. "You're filthy and stink. Even a Frog Island hussy has a right to say no."

The mindless grin disappeared from his face, replaced by a grimace of savage hate. Suggs grabbed her by the hair and slammed her to the floor. She groaned in pain. "When I'm done with you, sweetie,

I'm giving you to the boys out back. And I guarantee you that when we're done, you won't be talking so high and mighty." Struggling to regain control of himself, the grin creeping back onto his face like a mask, he continued in a fierce whisper again, pointing the cocked gun at Sally's head, "Now you kneel right there and you're gonna do just what I tell you. I want you to do me just the way I told you to before. Only this time you get paid by me letting you live a little longer." He unbuckled his belt and let his pants fall to the floor. "Now use your mouth for something other than sass."

Looking up at his face, contorted in anticipation, she concealed her revulsion and disgust, forcing to her face what she hoped would pass for a smile. Her only desperate hope for survival depended on this man lowering his guard for just a moment. Forgetting all else except his expected pleasure, the gun wavered in Sugg's hand.

"You know something, mister?" she said quietly, "I still say 'No!'." And before he could react she palmed the razor-sharp paring knife hidden up her sleeve and slammed it into his inner thigh, ripping it down and across as deeply as she could.

His eyes bulged in shock. Clutching the wound, he collapsed in the tangle of his bloody clothes. And then the pain hit him like a wall. He twisted and rolled, screaming, the blood gushing from his leg. Sally scrambled for the bag of ammo, but before she could gain it, another shadow fell across her from the doorway. "Suggs, what the devil…" Cob was struggling with the darkness also.

Knowing she had not a second to lose before his eyes would adjust, Sally spun and dashed past the man in the doorway. He saw someone fly by but reacted just a heartbeat too slow.

"Get her, Cob," Suggs begged weakly, trying to stem the flow of blood with his fingers, "It's that whore. She done cut me up bad." Cob backed a step into the sun and saw Sally sprinting across the yard toward the house, elbows pumping.

Dang these high-button shoes, she thought. *I'd a been better off barefoot.* She ran, expecting to feel a .45 slug slam into her back at any second. But Cob was now in hot pursuit, intent on closing with her. She ran as she hadn't in years, not since she raced against her brothers as a child. Her breath started coming in short gasps. Cob, finally realizing he would not catch her, braced his feet to better get off his shots.

"Get down, Sally, NOW!" She heard Mary's commanding voice and saw her friend standing on the porch, shouldering the shotgun. Without thinking, Sally dove as she heard the gun blast and felt hot pellets rip the air just over her head. "C'mon, gal. Get up," Mary urged. "Run!" Sally responded instantly. She staggered breathlessly the last few yards to the porch and through the door. Mary followed backing in, covering her with an empty gun.

As soon as Mary stepped in, Sally slammed the door shut behind her and dropped the bar across it. The door may not have been made of twelve inch thick oak, like Devil Anse's fort, but See Bird had made it solid, and it would take a mule to kick it in. Sally sagged onto a bench beside the door, her head held in her hands, utterly exhausted and depressed, as Mary took up her position beside the window. An occasional bullet from the shadows of the shed pinged harmlessly off the wall of the house. One hit and shattered the kitchen window, and through the gap the two women could hear incoherent shouting and swearing.

"I'm so sorry, Mary. But I failed. I completely failed. They found the shotgun shells, and there was one of 'em waiting in the shed. I could of got killed, and I could of got you killed too. It was a crazy idea. I'm so sorry. Now we got nothing." Sally rocked back and forth in her dismay.

"Pull yourself together, gal, and tell me what happened. Take your time. Them fools don't look like they're fixing to rush us anytime soon. Guess they've had about enough of this shotgun."

"Mama, can I come down? Are you okay?" Gertrude was watching her mother from the top of the ladder.

Sally stopped rocking back and forth and composed her face for her child. "You're right, of course, Mary. Yes, honey, mercy sakes, come here and give your ma a hug." Gertrude needed no urging. In a few seconds she was racing to her mother's arms again.

"Don't go out there anymore, Ma. It makes me too scared. I'm afraid those bad men will hurt you."

"Little Gertrude, don't you worry your pretty head on it. I don't figure there's any more reason to go out there 'til your Pap gets home. And from the looks of it, your Aunt Mary evened up the odds just a bit in our favor. Now, would you please go get me the hair brush from my bedroom. Your head looks like a rat's nest."

As the child, now reassured that all was well in her world, walked off to the bedroom, Sally told Mary about the scene in the shed, how close she had come to getting the bag of shells, and how she had stabbed Suggs with the paring knife she had slid up her sleeve. "I tried to go for the big artery running inside the leg. I'm not sure I got it. I couldn't stick around and find out."

Gertrude returned with the hairbrush and sat at her mother's feet while Sally brushed out the black curls.

"Mary, if I hadn't dove when I did," Sally reflected, "I do believe you'd of blown me to kingdom come."

"Sally, in a couple more seconds, he'd a had you dead for sure and I couldn't of got a shot off in time. Then we'd of been in a world of hurt. I had to believe you had the horse sense to duck when I told you to duck. And if I figure right, they was four what rode in here like they owned the place. Two ate lead, and one is pretty cut up if'n he ain't dead. I think we're doing pretty good for a mama and a widow woman. Let him come, if he got the nerve. There ain't no man what can match two hell-cats like us.

"Hell-cats. That's funny, Aunt Mary. Meow." Gertrude laughed a laugh that sounded like fast running water over stones in a brook.

"Shush now, Gertrude," Sally reprimanded, "don't you go saying things like that." But she said it with a smile. "Well, Mary, I've caught my wind now. So if you'd make sure the window shutters are all locked, except for the kitchen and this one here by the door, I think I'll cook us up some dinner. Maybe the smells of good cooking will drive that hawkshaw crazy and he'll shoot hisself. I'm so hungry my belly thinks my throat is cut."

The evening oranges and reds hung in the air like the mist that would drift up the slopes of the mountains and linger as though tethered to the treetops. But eventually that last shade disappeared from the sky, to be replaced by sharp, white pinpricks of light suspended on a black velvety background. The sliver of a crescent moon cast little light on the farm nestled in the hollow below. The hens had gone to roost. Fear rose in the breasts of the women as the silent blackness descended, but they did their best to hide it for the sake of the small child. Since the few random shots fired in their direction hours ago, silence wrapped itself around the house like a thick blanket.

In the loft, Sally sat on the edge of Gertrude's bed. Tucked as it was under the slope of the roof, she had to be mindful lest she smack her head against the ceiling. Reaching over, she stroked her child's hair and hummed a soft lullabye. "Sleep now, little one," she soothed as Gertrude rolled over on her side. "Your Pap will be home tomorrow, and everything will be just fine. We'll have us an egg hunt and bake up a rhubarb pie. Goodnight now. I'll come up and check on you in a bit." Leaning down, she placed a kiss as soft as a whisper on the little girl's forehead. "Good night, sleep tight, God bless you, and sweet dreams."

"Umm. G'night Ma."

Sally stood and looked out the window, hearing only the crickets and rhythmic peeping of the frogs down by the creek that tumbled through the hollow, detecting only the faintest glimmer of starlight off the porch roof below. *Where are you, See Bird?* she wondered. *I'm holding on here, but by the skin of my teeth. You were right. I should of done as you said and stayed up at Devil Anse's. Why do I buck you so much? I wish I knew.* She sighed to herself and carefully descended the ladder.

Mary had lit a lantern in the kitchen, its dim glow casting long shadows throughout house. With all the shutters locked shut and the door barred, the place felt more like a crypt than the bright and airy home it became during the day.

Neither woman wanted to sleep, but both needed it desperately. Desultory conversation tapered off and ceased. They sat in the area Sally had taken to call her 'parlor,' adjacent to her bedroom on the west side of the house. "I don't know what else we can do now but wait 'til dawn," Mary said finally, reclining on the settee and fluffing a pillow beneath her head. "Keep that knife handy, Sally. I'm gonna get me some shuteye. I'll spell you after a while." Sally just nodded her assent from the rocking chair.

She awoke with a start, all of her senses alert, her head clear. She had heard something, of that she was certain. But what was it? Perhaps it had just been Gertrude's bed squeaking as she tossed or turned in her sleep. Heavens knows how the child had remained so calm, given the terrible excitement of the day. But, no, there it was again, the kind of sound a person would make, walking on the porch and trying not to make a sound.

Sally glided over to where Mary slept and gently shook her shoulder. Mary opened her eyes and looked at Sally's face by the dim light. "Someone's outside," Sally whispered. "I heard him walking on the porch."

Mary swung her legs to the floor. "What are we gonna do?"

"I don't know, but look." Mary turned her face in the direction Sally indicated. The door latch turned and the door tightened against the bar as some outside force applied pressure. Then the door returned to its original position as the pressure against it ceased. A few moments later, the women started again and turned to face the shuttered window in the parlor as the slightest sound of boot on board riveted their eyes in that direction.

"He's testing the windows," Mary whispered. "But," she added with a reassurance she did not feel, "he'll not get in that way. They're all locked up tight."

"Not all of them," Sally said. "I'm cooking up some lard, soon's I get the fire built up."

"Lard," Mary questioned. "What for? The man cain't fly."

Sally said nothing but walked directly to the stove and soon had a large saucepan of melted lard bubbling away. After checking on it she stepped to the counter. "Mary, you take this large butcher knife," she directed, "and watch the windows. If you get a chance, stick it somewhere so's it'll hurt." She handed it to her friend and, using a towel for a hot pad, carefully removed the saucepan of scalding lard from the stove and carried it to the loft ladder. "But first help me with this hot pan. I'm going up. Then you hand it to me."

"Okay, Sal, but what on earth are you planning on cooking up there?"

"Maybe I'm worried about nothing, but this man Coburn don't give up easily. I plan on making the porch roof outside Gertrude's window so slick, he'd think twice about trying that window."

Mary nodded her understanding and passed the saucepan up to Sally. Probably it was worry for nothing, but doing anything was preferable to just sitting there, waiting for dawn. The women moving about and making noise wakened Gertrude. She sat up in her bed and asked, "What'cha doing ma?"

"You just go back to sleep, honey. It'll be day soon, and my, we'll have us some fun."

"But what'cha doing?" The curious child rose and stepped beside her mother at the window. Already the false dawn was throwing its deep purples and orange fringe into the sky.

"I'm just going to toss this lard out on the porch roof. The windows are all closed downstairs." She glanced at the slowly lightening sky. "It's sure a good thing your Pap didn't put any shutters on the upstairs windows, now isn't it?" She hurled the hot lard out onto the roof and stepped back, wondering if it had been a foolish act. Gertrude stepped up to the window, leaning out to see the results of what her mother had done.

A man's hand appeared, gripping the side of the window frame, followed immediately by his head. Startled, Gertrude let loose a high-pitched scream, but before she could move, the hand released its grip and, seeking blindly some other object to attach to, locked onto the girl's arm. Coburn's shocked face appeared as Gertrude screamed again. Sally lunged forward, but Coburn, with nothing to support himself, stepped up and onto the newly greased roof. Instantly his feet lost traction and he fell backwards, yanking the little girl through the open window. Sally's desperate hands closed on empty air where a moment before, her child had stood. "Gertrude!"

"Mama!" Gertrude screamed, and as her mother watched in horror, almost as though it were in slow motion, Coburn slid towards the edge of the roof, clutching the flailing child as if she would protect him or prevent his falling. His boot heels caught on the edge and he tumbled over backwards, releasing Gertrude with a curse. A moment later there was a terrible sound of bones crunching and splintering, followed by silence once again.

"Gertrude!" Sally yelled from the window. Without waiting for a response, she spun and raced down the ladder. By the time she hit the floor, Mary was unbarring the door. She had heard the commotion and deduced what had happened. Sally flung open the door and both women raced around the corner of the house.

Draped over the rain barrel was the body of a man, bent backwards at an impossible angle. Coburn had used it to climb up onto the porch roof, and it had caught him as he descended, shattering his spine and killing him instantly. But Sally and Mary spared barely a glance and not a thought for him. Their eyes focused on the small broken bundle that lay in the grass a few yards from the dead man. Sally fell to her knees beside her and called her name softly, over and over, soothingly, cooing like a dove. She caressed the small broken arms and huddled over her as though to detect any faintest whiff of a breath. Mary stood behind her, eyes wide in horror, her hand over her mouth, staring at this moonlit tableau of terror.

Sally's body hung over that of the child, as if by so doing she could offer the protection in death she failed to provide in the child's life. Her long hair draped the small body like a willow over the bank of a stream. Then her shoulders started convulsing, and the shaking spread to the rest of her body. "My baby's dead! Oh, God, my beautiful baby's dead!" The shaking became uncontrolled sobbing as Sally collapsed over the small broken body. "Gertrude, my darling little Gertrude." She forced herself back up to a kneeling position and once again held the now lifeless little limbs. "Oh, no. She's gone. Why couldn't it have been me? God, why not me?" Mary knelt by her side and wept, embracing her distraught friend by the shoulders, adding her tears to the stream that fell on the inert and broken body of the child.

7

The sun was nearing its peak in the sky as See Bird walked a tired Kiamichi up the slope on the final stretch of trail that would open on the hollow to his home. The sturdy horse had not complained, though he endured seven hours of hard riding through some of the most difficult terrain east of the Rockies. It was as if when God first made the world He created everywhere else first and then, before He lay down to rest, he shook out a fancy quilt and just let it lay where it fell, wrinkles everywhere and running in all directions – *That was West Virginia,* he thought.

He might have smiled at the image, but he was too exhausted from the journey. He dismounted to walk the horse periodically, giving both his and Kiamichi's backs a rest. Instead he quickly found himself running alongside the jogging horse, prodded by an irresistible urge to hurry, to waste not a single minute. Thankfully, Sally had packed his mocs. He couldn't imagine running far in his work boots. His sense of an imminent threat caused him to continually scan the forests on each side of the road and to leave the sheathed Winchester unstrapped. Though he detected nothing, as the hours sped by, his sense of danger and dread only increased.

Now, as he completed the final climb, knowing he soon would be in the company of those he loved, he worried himself with guilt and regret. He knew that in spite of Sally's resistance, he should have forced the issue and insisted she take refuge at her uncle's place until he would return. *What if something would have delayed him? Why did he clam up so tight within himself and not protect her in spite of herself?* His thoughts were broken by the soft sound of horses cropping grass nearby.

Instantly alert, See Bird dismounted and dropped the reins. Kiamichi would not wander off. The quarter horse had been trained to wait for a command, and See Bird knew the steed would do just that. Silently sliding the Winchester out of its saddle scabbard, he slipped through the trees off the trail as the woods opened on his homestead.

Four horses stood at the edge of the clearing, by the creek, grazing as peacefully as if they lived there. But their riders were nowhere to be seen. See Bird edged along the wood line. Every fiber in his being wanted to race across the gap between him and the house, sitting placidly in the hollow before and slightly below him, its door wide open. But he knew that a wrong move here could be fatal and guessed the horses left up here and not down by the house bade only the worst. As he approached the back side of the shed he stopped and brought up his rifle. An area of flattened grass marked what could only have been used as a camping area. As a matter of fact, See Bird noticed, someone was asleep on his stomach, partially concealed beneath a blanket.

He levered a round into the Winchester but the sleeping man did not stir. Cautiously See Bird stepped forward, studying the prone body. Sensing no movement, he lifted the edge of the blanket with the rifle barrel and flicked it off. Whoever it was, based on the multiple wounds he had suffered, See Bird was sure the man would never wake again, at least not in this life. It was obvious his backside had borne the brunt of a shotgun blast at short range. But how had he then gotten here?

Slowly, the young Choctaw turned the corner of the shed and stepped inside. From the corner of his eyes he detected movement on the floor against the far wall and heard a soft moan. Winchester at the ready, he advanced into the shadows. He nearly slipped in a pool of congealing blood. There, at his feet, lay a half-naked man, barely conscious, moaning in pain, a pistol resting in one hand on the floor, while with the other hand he was trying futilely to stem the blood flow from a deep slash across the inside of his thigh. His pants lay crumpled and twisted about his feet. It was obvious the man would be dead soon without immediate medical attention, and See Bird doubted even that would help.

"Help me, mister," the wounded man moaned. He tried but failed to lift the pistol. See Bird recognized him as the big grinner from the visit of Coburn and his bounty hunters just the other day.

"What happened?" See Bird asked as he stepped on the man's pistol hand, forcing it to the floor.

The wounded man groaned again, too weak to remove his hand from beneath See Bird's boot. His focus seemed to wander for a moment and the hand trying to stem the softly pulsing blood flow fumbled about the gaping slash. "That damned little whore," he mumbled. See Bird stiffened as he realized who the man was talking about. "She cut me open like a pig. I was just gonna have me a little fun. I'll kill the…"

"You're not going to kill anyone," See Bird whispered. He moved his foot off the man's gun hand and kicked the pistol across the floor. He backed a step toward the door.

Seeing his only chance of survival leaving, Suggs rallied himself once more. "Help me, I don't want to die," he begged feebly.

See Bird hesitated in the door and then stepped back to the man's side. Squatting down and cradling the Winchester across his lap, he watched as the last pulses of the blood flow stopped. "You're already dead," he whispered. "Now, go to hell."

A slight breeze caught the door of the shed and swung it open. Out of the corner of his eye, See Bird caught the movement and swung around suddenly, nearly firing at it. His nerves were heightened and drawn to the breaking point. There were four horses and four men. Two were accounted for. Clearly Sally had been out here but must have escaped after fatally wounding this man. Had the other two rushed the house? Were they even now lying in wait, peering out of the open door at him? The windows were all shuttered – but the door stood wide open. What did it all mean? In spite of a growing sense of urgency, he crouched at the shed door and sprinted over to the same garden fence Sally used as cover the day before. A crumpled bundle of what must certainly be a person lay sprawled only paces from the porch. Too large for either woman, it had to be another of the bounty hunters. It now seemed evident they had rushed the house, and it also seemed evident the two women had taken a heavy toll of the attackers. Four horses – three bodies. Only one man remained unaccounted for. But if he had reached the house, even now Sally, Mary, and Gertrude could be in extreme peril. A wrong move on his part and they all could be killed by a desperado such as Coburn or one of his henchmen.

Since all the windows were shuttered See Bird felt he could risk a sprint around the back of the house in order to gain the porch. In a silent crouch, his finger resting on the Winchester's trigger-guard, he raced behind the garden fence and then along the back of the house. He stopped to catch his breath with his back to the wall at the corner, brought the rifle up to ready, and swung around the corner. He was staggered by what he saw: Draped over the rain barrel at an impossible angle was the grotesquely bent form of Coburn himself. His face stared out at nothing, frozen into the mask of horror he wore at the moment of his death.

See Bird was stunned by the carnage he was witness to, yet his face gave no clue as to his feelings. He felt no sense of relief in the knowledge that somehow Mary and Sally had tackled and beaten incredible odds. Overriding all his thoughts was one of puzzlement – *If all four of the men were dead, why were things so quiet, and why was the door standing open with the windows shuttered? Had they all left, perhaps to the security of a neighbor?*

See Bird reconciled himself to the idea that, indeed, the women most likely had, after what must have been a terrible ordeal, left to wait for him elsewhere. Relaxing, he slowly turned the corner of the porch and stepped into the open doorway. His initial impression was one of almost churchlike serenity. The only light, other than through the door in which he stood, beneath the low-slung porch, flowed in via the two second-story windows below the peaks at either end of the house. In the softly filtered light he recognized the two women, Sally and Mary, standing by the kitchen table with their backs to him. For some unknown reason, Sally was wearing his clothes. Though he should have called out to his wife, the sense of dread and oppression he had felt all day washed over him like a flood, submerging his normal reactions. He found himself not wanting to see what they were looking at on the table. They must have heard him enter because Mary and then Sally slowly turned to look at him.

Mary's face was lined with grief, but she had recently lost a husband. His gaze turned to Sally. In her eyes he saw an inexpressible grief, the evidence of a deeply wounded soul. She raised her hands to him as if in offering, "My baby's gone," she whispered. "Them murderers killed her." Overwhelmed by the realization of what she had said, Sally sank to her knees, dropping her hands to her sides, too weak to hold up her head. Mary knelt beside her, cradling her and rocking back and forth, as if to console a small child. On the table behind them, now clearly visible even in the dimness of the house, lay Gertrude, dressed all in white, in death as cold and pale as a China Doll. The women had been preparing her body for burial.

A guttural "No" was all See Bird could choke out. Dropping the rifle, he strode slowly, like a sleepwalker toward the tableau at the kitchen table. Now he knew, now he understood why before dawn he had suddenly awakened from troubled dreams. Now he understood the compulsion which forced him to push Kiamichi to his limits. Now he simply understood.

But the 'why' of it all eluded him. Was he driven so hard just to get home in time to bury this child and watch the woman he had grown to love dissolve in despair? Was the God of the universe a diabolically cruel being who delighted in doling out to man a tiny dollop of joy, only to snatch it away and feed Himself off His creatures' pain? As he faced his doubt it seemed as though an endless black abyss opened before him. He balanced on its lip.

No, he thought. *This is a lie. I was brought here*

for a reason. Feeling as empty as a barren canyon through which the only sound is the lonely whistling of the desert wind, See Bird walked forward and lifted the small child. Her skin was as cold and smooth as a polished stone plucked from a stream bed. He felt, more than saw, the two women rise and stand at his side. *I am empty,* he thought, *I have nothing. I am nothing,* he prayed. *It's all you. Do what you will, for your own sake.*

The room dimmed, as if the house were passing beneath a heavy cloud, or as if in the presence of some unseen force. See Bird cradled the child in one arm. With the other he lovingly stroked her hair. With a finger he traced a line down her face, across her ivory cold forehead, along the border of her eyebrow, touching ever so lightly, Gertrude's eyelashes. From her cheek, across her soft lips, her chin, neck, and shoulders, he continued until he enfolded her tiny white feet in his callused brown hand. He thought for a moment he was imagining the slightest movement, a twitch in one of her toes, then he felt it again. Releasing her foot, he traced the part in her curly black hair, drew his hand gently back down to her shoulders once again, tenderly gliding his hand down her arms, feeling, he imagined, the sinews and muscles warm to the touch. To Sally he may have appeared dreamy and unfocused, but never in his life had he felt so totally absorbed.

He felt a growing certainty that Gertrude lived, and feeling his legs growing weak, he lowered himself to a kneeling position, still cradling the child. Sally, sensing a change in her husband's demeanor from deep pain to something akin to hope, knelt to face him, sensing his exhaustion and leaned her head on his shoulder, as if by so doing she could give him strength. She reached to support her baby. His free hand again swept down, seemingly involuntarily and caressed the small form, more confidently, this time. Sally felt a slight movement and whimpered, drawing her child to her bosom. See Bird released the child into her mother's arms, cupped Gertrude's face, and leaned in to kiss her forehead, felt its warmth, and heard a tiny sigh.

All three adults noticed the light in the room growing denser, yet rich with a golden hue. An inexpressibly sweet fragrance delighted and refreshed them. See Bird heard what sounded like the tinkling of the tiniest and purest crystal bells. Then he felt his emptiness being filled to overflowing with peace, healing and well-being. The stream became a flood that swamped every pore in his body and then overflowed, through his arms, wrists, hands, and fingertips into the tiny body. His hands glided ever more slowly across Gertrude's form. Beneath them the warmth of life flowed again through her veins.

Color surged with returning life. Icy blue lips turned pink, and pale cheeks blushed. The three stared in amazement at the reanimated child. See Bird's hands came to rest on her chest. Then he felt it, the unmistakable beating of her heart, and a moment later his hands were visibly raised as Gertrude's lungs filled with air for the first time in hours. Sally moaned again, abandoning disbelief and embracing hope, cradled the child's head in her arms and cooing as she rocked back and forth.

Gertrude shivered, her eyelids flickered and opened, and darted about, taking in the scene. She focused on her mother's eyes. "Hi, Ma," she said, as though waking from a deep sleep, reaching up to touch her face. "What happened? How did I get here? Why are you crying?" Sally began laughing but the tears kept flowing. Mary stared, as though frozen, her hand covering her mouth.

The cloud enveloping the house passed on, and the room lightened again. See Bird watched dust motes floating in the rays of light that streamed through the upper window. Whatever or whoever had been there had moved on, leaving them as before, only not as they had ever been before.

See Bird raised his hands and looked at them. Nothing special, callused from hard physical labor, there was not a thing to distinguish them from anyone else's. He flexed his fingers and walked over to the bench by the door. Sitting down, he picked up his rifle where he dropped it and propped it against the wall. Leaning back, he closed his eyes to rest, and immediately fell into a deep and restful sleep, Sally's joyful laughter, like a song, the last sound he heard.

8

What exactly transpired that summer's day in the little house in Warm Hollow became the subject of intense speculation. See Bird, not one to indulge himself in gossip or puffery, averred with all sincerity, that he had done nothing at all and never broached the subject again. Sally, normally as garrulous as a magpie, respected See Bird's desire the subject be kept private between the two of them. In any case, she was living in such an elevated state of joy at getting her daughter back from the dead, that to speak of it with others seemed to trivialize its magnitude. Gertrude remembered nothing, from the moment she was standing at her bedroom window in her night dress until she woke on the kitchen table as though from a deep sleep, dressed as if she were going to a party.

It was Mary who carried the story from pie socials to church gatherings to neighbors visiting neighbors. That something strange had happened was never in doubt. Two mountain women dispatched four vicious bounty hunters with only two shotgun shells. If that wasn't a miracle then one didn't exist. But as to what happened to little Gertrude, on that opinions differed. Some believed that, with See Bird's laying on of hands, God had in fact raised her from the dead. Others believed when she had been flung out of the window, the child had hit her head, knocking her out, and See Bird, by manipulating and massaging her body had stimulated her recovery. The two women, so this interpretation went, distraught by the ordeal they endured, simply misinterpreted events. Others referred to Red's mysterious origins and hinted of black magic. Whatever the truth, since See Bird and Sally refused to talk about it, after a while mountain folk did what they usually do in such cases – they shrugged their shoulders, respected their neighbor's privacy, and went on with the struggle for daily survival, chalking the strange event up as just another inexplicable mystery of the mountains.

By mid-summer, life had settled into a welcome routine again. Sally cultivated her garden until it was the envy of the neighborhood. She worked it daily, weeding, hoeing, and teaching Gertrude the difference between the weeds needing to be pulled and plants needing nurture. This after one episode where Sally turned around in the garden from her work to see Gertrude standing there with a handful of young carrots she had just yanked, having mistaken them for weeds. The health of the family depended on Sally's diligence. What wasn't eaten as fresh harvest was canned or stored for the winter. But on many a day, when the house was in order and the garden needed no tending, See Bird would see the two ladies of the house in their bonnets tripping off to the woods to pick blackberries and hunt for herbs or wildflowers that would later grace the parlor with their fragrance and a touch of beauty.

See Bird, the ex-cowboy, took to farming with a vengeance, hoping to build not just a successful farm but also his enthusiasm. Besides the shed, a small barn rose to house the pair of milk cows and the two sows and a boar he had purchased from Jerry Hatfield. Like almost everyone else in the neighborhood, he rose early, before the rooster crowed, and didn't stop until Sally called him in for supper. It was too late in the summer to plant any crops this year but he still had a little of his original stake. With it he intended next spring to put a section of acreage into tobacco as his cash crop. More and more, as word of his prowess with iron, wood, and leather spread, he found himself taking on jobs fixing or building wagons or perhaps just their wheels for much needed cash.

He sometimes regretted using Kiamichi as a plow horse and thought as soon as he could he would buy or trade for a mule. On occasion, of an evening, he would saddle up and the two would gallop off for a brisk ride through the countryside. When he returned, Sally noticed both man and horse seemed so much more refreshed and happier.

Whatever entertainment they enjoyed was manufactured there on the farm. One evening, as the three sat on the front porch swing, with Gertrude prattling on about her day, Sally pulled a harmonica from her pocket and held it up for both of them to see.

"What is it, ma?" the child asked, her eyes brimming with fascination at the shiny thing before her. She reached for it but Sally pulled it away.

"This is a mouth organ, child, and it makes music. I ran across it today at the bottom of a box I packed years ago."

See Bird looked at her in surprise. "I didn't know you could play," he said.

Sally assumed her most mysterious face and said, "There's much you don't know about me, Bird." She winked and added, "I can play me a mean juice harp too."

"Well, then, let's hear something lively, gal."

With that, Sally blew the scales out and rapped the harmonica in the palm of her hand. Gertrude's eyes went wide and she sat up straighter. Sally placed the mouth organ back to her lips and launched into 'Wildwood Flower.' Gertrude clapped her hands. See Bird watched and listened for a moment, then slowly rose as though he was going to go into the house, but instead he tucked his thumbs into his belt, and to Gertrude's amazement went thumping past, feet clogging in perfect time to the music. Finally, unable to stand it any longer, the little girl jumped up and grabbed her Pap's hands. Watching what he was doing, she tried to control her feet and imitate the action. Excitement overcame her after only a minute or two and she released his hands and jumped around in happy circles.

"I didn't know you could dance like that," Sally commented to him after the song ended and he sat back down beside her.

With a sly squint, See Bird winked and said, "There's a lot you don't know about me, gal." He leaned back, satisfied with himself and retrieved a piece of wood that was well on its way to becoming a horse in the act of lunging forward, and after rotating it a few times, went to work on it with his big knife, humming Sally's song quietly to himself.

And so the evening and the days passed.

The local patrol Devil Anse initiated made its rounds swinging by nearly every other day, for a while. But as autumn deepened, the pace of life in the mountains quickened. Hogs had to be slaughtered, crops harvested, and all of it put up for the winter. The patrols gradually ceased altogether. That did not mean folks were any less diligent. See Bird kept his Winchester handy, and neighbors looked out for each other. Among themselves, the mountain inhabitants were as cordial and sociable as ever. But many a stranger, wandering through, stopping at some cabin in the hills to seek directions, felt the chill of their distrust.

One crisp September morning while the family was having a breakfast of fried oats and fresh biscuits with bacon, they were called to the door by Devil Anse himself. "Good morning, folks," he smiled from the back of his horse. Good thing I et a'ready, Sal. That smells finer'n anything."

"Uncle Devil Anse," Sally called, "you just git yourself down here and have some coffee. There's a nip to the air, and it'll warm you up good."

The clan leader swung his leg over the horse's back and jumped off as nimbly as a man half his age. See Bird admired the comfortable way that man sat a horse. Rumor was that Devil Anse was the best horseman and shot in this part of West Virginia and Kentucky. See Bird did not for a moment doubt it. "Good coffee is something I can never walk away from, gal. So I don't care if I do." Sally stood on her tiptoes on the porch and still had to reach up to give her uncle a hug around the neck.

Once everyone was seated around the table and Gertrude found her nesting spot on Devil Anse's lap, Sally placed the coffee pot on the table for the men to help themselves. As Devil Anse began, little Gertrude played in his full beard with her chubby fingers. Seemingly inured to such shenanigans he ignored her distractions. Before long she tucked her head against his chest and, parting the beard with her hands, poked her face out for a moment and then disappeared behind it again.

"Red," he said, "I figure on getting' in some bear hunting today. I h'aint been out all year, what with the troubles and all. The boys are all busy. So Levicy suggested I come a calling and see if you might be interested. What do you say?"

See Bird sat back, cradling the hot cup in his hands, watching Gertrude play in this fierce man's beard. *It was funny,* he thought, *how these people could seem so stern and unbending, and yet tolerate, welcome even the attentions of small children. Devil Anse could not have imagined how downright silly he looked with Gertrude peeking out from behind his beard with him planning a bear hunt.* That was one thing about mountain folk See Bird responded to, their unfeigned delight in children and the respect they paid their elders. Gertrude made a funny face at her Pap and then disappeared again behind the mass of curly black hair. "I've hunted plenty in my time, Devil Anse. On the cattle trail, antelope and prairie chicken were standard fare. Occasionally I had me the opportunity to shoot something bigger. Since I been here, the game has been mostly coons, possums, and maybe a white tail or two." He paused to consider, then set the cup down. "Count me in," he said. "That is if Gertrude there and Sally can hold down the fort. What chores I got to do can wait for one day, at least."

Devil Anse beamed. "There ain't nothing like bear, old son. 'Course there's some folks what hold it might be a bit gamy. But this time of the year ol' bruin has gobbled up so many berries and sweet things, getting' ready for his winter nap, that I prefer it to venison, 'specially if he ain't too old."

"Well then, what are you two runnin' on your chops about?" Sally interrupted. "We sure could use the meat and cooking lard, so the sooner you get goin' the sooner you'll get back. 'Sides that, I got me some quilts to work on, and I can't hardly do it with you yammerin' men under foot."

See Bird and Sally walked out to the front porch side by side, their arms around each other's waists. Devil Anse extricated Gertrude from the tangle of his beard and now bounced the chattering youngster along on his back just behind them. "Sally," See Bird spoke softly, "if you don't want me to go I won't."

"Why on earth not, Bird?"

It's just that the last time I was gone… you know what I mean. I'm just not sure it's the right time."

She pulled him just a bit closer so that their hips locked in rhythm as they walked. "That's real sweet of you, darling," she said and gave his cheek a peck. "But I'm a big girl. What kind of woman would I be that couldn't let her man out of her sight? Not that I want you to be out of my sight for very long." He said nothing as they stood on the porch together, facing each other. "Besides, in case you hadn't noticed, I think someone's watching over us. So I won't fret. You go now," she gently pushed at him, "and bring us home some meat for the winter."

See Bird held her close for a moment and then released her. Stooping, he hoisted up Gertrude and gave her a kiss on her forehead. "Be a good girl now, little darlin'," he said and deposited her gently on the ground. "Devil Anse," he said, "it'll only take me a minute to saddle up and get me a box of .44s. I'll be right back." See Bird hurried off toward the small barn and corral. Kiamichi, sensing his excitement, greeted him at the gate with a whinny.

Later that morning, the two men rode slowly up a switchback trail high in the hills. Autumn came earlier up here than it did down in the lower elevations, the hollows and the Ohio River valley. Up here where the air was clearer and cooler, the poplar's leaves were just beginning their slow fade to pale yellow and green.

Then, almost all at once the maples would explode in a riot of red- oranges, and the oaks would add their coppers. They rode single file with Devil Anse leading, sometimes up a slope to follow a ridge line, then down onto a saddle between peaks before starting up another ridge yet again. Always, they rode higher than before. See Bird noted that it had been several hours since they last had seen trace of human habitation, and that only an ancient collapsed cabin overgrown with wild scrub. Finally, when See Bird was wondering if they were going to travel all day, Devil Anse rounded a knob on a trail that must have been used only by game and drew his horse to a halt. See Bird drew alongside of him and looked where the patriarch was gazing.

"Down there," the older man gestured with his head, "that's where we find the big boy." Stretching out before and below them, running roughly several miles between steep, forested slopes, lay a tangled mass, a hollow that really was no more than a jungled up ravine of dense undergrowth and tumbled rocks. Through it cut a small but noisy creek whose bubbling song could be detected even up where the two riders sat. After a moment's reflection, Devil Anse continued. "I know he's there. A couple years ago I brought some hounds with me to hunt that very cove. They picked up the scent right quickly and headed off up that creek," He pointed. "I followed but it's so thick it took me a while to catch up. I heard them up ahead, and I knew they had 'im cornered. I tried to call them off, but they most likely couldn't hear, what with all the baying and roaring going on. When I caught up to 'em things had quieted down quite a bit. Three of my best hounds were killed, tossed around like they was rag dolls, and three more were so busted up I had to put them out of their misery. Other than some blood and gobs of hair, there was no sign of old bruin. I left and ain't been back, figured I'd wait until he forgot about me. I know he's there, I can feel him. And this time there won't be no hounds to get in the way." He turned to See Bird and nodded, "You bring that Winchester with you. Might be you'll get an open shot. If you do, take it. He'll be bigger than you think, and it will take something powerful to stop 'im." Devil Anse pulled a massive pistol out of his holster and checked the chamber. "I figure as thick as that mess down there is, I might not have room for a rifle. But by God, this 7mm will stop anything that walks on dry land." He settled it back in its holster and looked at See Bird. "Red," he said quietly, "I must have shot over two hundred bear in my time, and who knows how many other creatures. And I can honestly say I never once killed me anything on this earth for the pleasure of it, neither man nor beast. But seeing the terrible mess that creature made of those dogs," he shook his head as if revisiting an unpleasant memory – "bruin seemed to me like that he cornered them, rather than the other way around, and just slaughtered them. I can still hear his roaring like boulders rolling down a mountain." He paused again and then with added intensity said, "He was enjoying it, Red. He was getting the thrill of a lifetime out of killing them dogs the way he did.

"I never forgot it, but I told the boys when I got home that the pack just took off. They do that sometimes." Devil Anse dismounted and dug out more shells to fill his pockets. "I didn't want those boys to get hurt back here. They don't know this bear like I do.

"So we'll leave the horses up here. They'll be safe, and we hoof it in from here." The mountaineer in the tall boots started hiking down the slope to the bottom of the ravine, See Bird one step behind in his mocs. "Before the sun sets today, that bear will be dead – either that or I will. But I don't expect that will be the case."

Near the bottom, they came to a halt as Devil Anse examined a tree. "Look at these claw marks, Red," he said, examining the length and depth of gouges in the bark just over his head. "This'll give you some idea of how big he is. If he stands up and charges, I say again don't hesitate a second. Aim for body cavities. Odds are we won't kill him first try, but we gotta hurt him enough so he don't outrun us and get away."

See Bird imagined size required to make such marks, and wondered if maybe .165 grains might not be enough. This bear would be big enough to yank a man right out of the saddle, or to take down the horse itself.

The two hunters started up the ravine, one on either side of the creek, checking for any sign of their prey. For the size of the beast, it left remarkably little trace, a hair caught on a bramble here, a broken twig there. What there was no chance of missing was the huge pile of bear scat See Bird cautiously circled. What scant breeze there was, when there was any air movement at all, seemed to be flowing down the ravine, into their faces. That, at least, they had in their favor. Though it was scarcely past noon, the sun had already crept behind the ridgeline to the west, leaving them in deepening shadows. A number of times See Bird found himself stopped, staring into some brambles ahead, wondering if the shade concealed some more ominous presence. The hairs on his arms began to prickle and stand as his increasing sense of vulnerability and danger strengthened.

Finally, he waved Devil Anse over to a halt and walked up to him. Devil Anse looked at him expectantly. See Bird noticed and responded, "No, I can't see anything. But something big has been through here recently. I'm starting to feel like one of your hounds, and I don't like it a bit. He knows every bend, bush, and boulder, and we can barely see our hands in front of our faces."

"You're right about that, Red," Devil Anse said. "If I remember right, we're getting near to where that bear ambushed my dogs last time. 'Course with this mess, it's hard to be sure. I'm feeling the willies a mite too. What do you suggest?"

"This might seem crazy, but I don't think it's any less than the way we're going now. I want to get up a little higher, along that slope over there. From there I can keep an eye on you easily enough, and if he is down here, maybe I can spot him and give a warning. You watch for any signal from me. How's that sound?"

Devil Anse considered the proposition for a few moments. He did not relish the idea of splitting up. However, he relished even less the prospect of rounding some bend or fighting out of some brambles only to be charged at point blank range. Finally he nodded and whispered, "That's as good a plan as any. Just try to stay in sight. I don't want to shoot you by accident, and sure as moonshine I don't want you to mistake me for a bar." He smiled, See Bird nodded and turned to recross the stream.

Devil Anse waited until his partner had scaled the slope opposite him and was up about forty feet, where the brush appeared to thin out some. Unfortunately, the terrain See Bird had to traverse was made more difficult due to sudden and unpredictable outcroppings of rocks which would force him to lose time going up and over them or down and around them. But in such manner the two men struggled forward, ever more slowly.

At one place where some boulders the size of small cabins had broken off encroaching walls and tumbled into the stream, the creek itself was diverted into a large loop. Where several large trees had slid down, See Bird could see Devil Anse clearly as the mountaineer cautiously made his way upstream. Rather than descend and uselessly follow the new stream course, he decided to cut off the loop and meet Devil Anse on the other side. He was leaning on a boulder, about to step over it when one of the boulders below seemed to move. And then there was no doubt about it. Although he hadn't sensed See Bird's presence, Bruin knew someone was approaching from downstream and began his charge. Devil Anse would be completely unaware of what would shortly burst around the corner and be on him before he could draw his gun.

See Bird yelled for all he was worth, hoping Devil Anse could hear him. The bear below took no notice of the man above, if in its focus, it heard him at all. Its slow lumbering gait became gallop, eating up the one hundred or so yards to the corner of the stream in seconds. As large as a steer, the bear could move as fast as one. Now it seemed to fly down the stream, gliding over the stones. See Bird had no time to devise a plan. His decisions had to be right and they had to be made in the instant. Seeing no chance for a shot, he dropped the rifle and raced along the rocks for the corner the bear was about to round. With his left hand he snatched his Arkansas Toothpick from its scabbard behind his hip. He gained the corner a moment behind the massive bear only to see him rear up as it spotted its puny human prey standing in the stream before it.

Devil Anse, if he felt his death staring him in the face, faced it manfully. Taking a few slow steps backward, he drew his pistol, and as the bear strode around the corner, howling in rage, stood one leg slightly before the other, and held the pistol directly before him, left hand over right, and fired directly into the towering bear's chest. The rocks echoed with the report. If bruin felt the massive slug it gave no indication and advanced another step. Devil Anse retreated a few feet, braced himself and fired again. Roaring in its pain and frustration, the bear advanced, now but a few yards in front of him. Devil Anse was almost within range of its scimitar-like claws and heard its breathing and smelled its hot breath. Hesitating not for a second, See Bird leaped into the air, his knife descending even as he crashed onto the back of the bear. Firmly seated, knotting a handful of black hair as he would a bronc's mane, he slammed the knife down into the brute's back. It hesitated, as if for the first time feeling pain. It wavered and looked to turn and swipe the tormenting figure from its back. See Bird raised the big knife and smashed it down again, this time releasing his grip on the bear in order to use both hands to drive the big blade deep. Bruin made a feeble attempt to turn and face him, staggered, lost its balance and crashed to the ground just feet from where Devil Anse stood, his pistol still aimed directly at the beast. See Bird leaped off just in time to avoid being crushed and rolled to his feet, wielding only his knife, in a knife-fighter's stance, gasping for air but ready to go another round.

Both men stared in wonder at the suddenly inert behemoth. Devil Anse spoke first as he walked slowly around the body, gun still at the ready. "If I had known the size of this critter, I probably would have stayed home. You must have knifed it in the heart, for it to drop like that. Good Lord," he said in awe, "look at the size of that head. How big do you reckon him to be?"

See Bird relaxed and drew in a long breath, the knife dangling in his hand. "I can't be sure, but I'm guessing he'd tip the scales at near a thousand pounds."

After making a complete circuit of the animal, never removing the aim of the big gun from its head, slowly Devil Anse lowered his gun and slipped it back into its holster. "I think you're right. Sally and Levicy will be in bear grease for the winter now." He took his eyes off the shiny black mound and eyed See Bird appreciatively. "I heard you yell and figured to get ready. If you hadn't jumped it like you did Levicy'd be a widow about now, and Gertrude wouldn't have my beard to play hide-and-seek in."

See Bird nodded, feeling embarrassed at the gratitude being expressed. He had not made any conscious decision in the last five minutes. His reactions had been entirely instinctive, and if he had the time now to think it over, he was not sure he would make the same choices. Had he not leaped onto the bear's back like he did, perhaps Devil Anse would have had time for one more shot. And maybe that shot would have brought the beast down. Maybe. He shrugged inwardly. "I'll go get the horses and make a travois to drag the carcass out. Why don't you start in on butchering, so's we can lug this carcass outta here and get on home? I don't fancy sticking 'round here any longer than I have to." He surveyed the tangled walls around them.

"Sounds good to me, Red. I'm an old man and tired of walking anyways." With that he pulled his knife and set to work, looking like anything but a tired old man. See Bird smiled and after retrieving his rifle headed back down the way they had come.

Later that afternoon, though the shadows stretched deep and dark down in the ravine, the two riders were surprised at how light it was up on the ridge. The sun was still hours from setting, and the two rode along contentedly, wrapped in their own thoughts. Once, when they came to a brief halt beside another small stream to give their steeds a blow, Devil Anse spoke. "I been riding and thinking, Red. This land is too grand for us measly humans to be carrying on the way we are. It deserves better."

"Makes sense to me, Devil Anse. What are you thinking?"

"Only there didn't always used to be a feud going on. During The War Between The States Ran'l McCoy and me both served in the same unit and both cut out at the same time. We came home and formed the Logan Wildcats, a ranger group to drive the Yankees out of these hills. You being a youngster from out west, you might not of heard much about it."

"Yes sir," See Bird replied. "I did. Lots of our people, the Choctaw filled the Confederate ranks. There was no love lost between us and the US government. It drove us out of our lands, beautiful lands, like dogs in winter. Many of us died before ever reaching Oklahoma. In my family, Uncle Isaac went off to war, and he returned just in time to deliver me and my brother See Right. He taught me most everything useful that I know. He taught me when it was time to fight, and when it was time to let go of fighting." See Bird became still, and the two rode so that the only sound was the rhythmic clop of the horses' hooves and the scraping of the heavily laden travois, dragging behind the horses.

Devil Anse broke the silence. "So you're saying this may be the time to let go the fighting?"

See Bird shrugged, "Could be," was all he said.

"Or maybe it's long past the time to let go the fighting."

They could have pushed on and maybe made it back to the farm by sunset, but the day had gone so well, and the weather was so sparkling, the two men decided to eat supper on the trail. See Bird quickly started a small fire and got some coffee boiling while Devil Anse cut off a couple bear steaks and spitted them over the flame. As they sizzled he said to See Bird, "When we came back from the War we were determined to rid the area of Yanks, like I said. Most Hatfields lived over here in West Virginia, and some in Kentucky. Most McCoys lived in Kentucky with a few over here. Although almost no Hatfields sided with the blue-bellies, quite a few of the Kentucky McCoys did. One fella, a Yankee named Asa McCoy, being wounded, was sent home to recuperate. Knowing he was close kin to Ran'l, I warned him to get out or get paid a visit. I would've rocked him some and probably dumped him on the other side of the Big Sandy. But he headed up into the hills and hid in a cave. We tracked him in the snow, but warn't nobody foolish enough to walk into a dark cave where there was an armed soldier. So I decided to have the boys fire a volley into the cave to drive him out."

He paused to turn the spit. "These steaks is about done. Anyway, as luck would have it, one of those random shots hit and killed the man." He removed a juicy steak and handed it to See Bird. "This one's yours. I like mine with a touch of cinders." He chuckled. "Ran'l nor any of the other McCoys made a big deal about it. I guess they kinda figured he had it coming. But it ate at Ran'l just the same. A man could tell if he knew where to look. And things kinda went downhill from there."

See Bird listened to the confession, if that's what it was, without interrupting. "Good steak," was all he said.

The late September sun was settling in flames over a western ridge as they broke camp for the final leg home, arriving after dark, tired but contented with the day's work. As they approached the farm house, it seemed to See Bird that the place overflowed with light streaming out every window and pouring through the open door. They must have been heard as a small voice announced their arrival excitedly, “Ma, ma, Pap and Uncle Devil Anse is home. They’re home.”

9

Colorful October became bleak November as it does in the mountains. Soggy greys and browns replaced the crimsons and blaze orange. Boots caked with red clay a half-inch thick stood outside the door as cold autumn rains swept up the hollows and in climbing the ridges dropped their burden as snow on the upper elevations. Gertrude watched it all from her upstairs window and marked off each day on a paper calendar she had made, with Sally's help, in order to count down the days to Christmas. She was not sure what it all meant, but it seemed very important to her parents. Though the harvest tempo had slowed considerably, life was still busy at the farm in Warm Hollow.

Chores had to be done every day. See Bird divided the barn into two sections – a smaller section for the sow and boar, and a larger one for the mule, two milk cows, Kiamichi and a mare. The chickens roosted where they could and usually lay their eggs in a shelf of nests he built for them. Upstairs was piled hay and bedding that also would serve as insulation for the animals below during the cold winter months. He spent much of his day in the barn and the workshed. Still, he found time to exercise the horses daily. Kiamichi, especially, seemed to look forward to their jaunts about the countryside, whinnying at the fence by the gate if See Bird delayed longer than the horse thought necessary.

Sally taught Gertrude how to knit, and not surprisingly the small child took to it rapidly. Her nimble little fingers quickly learned to manipulate the needles until she could sit and knit with Sally and chat at the same time. Although she was still quite young she found her place in the family by doing whatever she was found capable of. One of her chores was to collect eggs, which she did daily and with carefully controlled enthusiasm. If she found a nest which looked as though it could use more bedding, she would stuff more in and pat it down, all the while speaking softly to her clucking charges.

News was garnered from the occasional traveler passing by or from neighbors stopping in usually on their way to somewhere else. Sally always made it a special occasion. She would scurry about the kitchen, serving up fresh biscuits, a slice of leftover cake, or a slab of pie, and always plenty of coffee. It was on one such occasion they learned that Cap had been broken out of jail over in Upland. He had become a celebrity, with folks coming from all around, crowding into the small jail to hear him retell the story of his exploits. He was sentenced to one year in jail and had served several months of it when one night some sympathetic fellows using a sledge hammer and an axe, smashed in the brick wall of his cell from the outside. He had become so popular in the area that the law had not even bothered to go look for him. As long as he stayed out of trouble and out of its hair he was a free man.

The other eight men involved in the raid that left Alifair and her brother dead were not so fortunate. Over a second cup of coffee with Shelby Hatfield one afternoon, See Bird and Sally learned they were sent back to Pikeville, Kentucky, where, following a decision by the United States Supreme Court that even men captured illegally could be tried by the state, seven men were sentenced to life in prison and Ellison Mounts, known as Cottontop, was hung.

"Yes, indeed," Shelby said, "Hanging Cottontop was the best entertainment folks around there have had in ages. They say over 5,000 showed up. The militia had to be called up to control the crowd." Gulping down a slice of Sally's double chocolate cake, he continued, "It's a crying shame to treat a man's death, even if he deserved it, like it's some gol-danged circus. Police and militia were everywhere. Rumors was flying that even as Cottontop was being marched to the gallows, Devil Anse himself was riding at the head of a hundred vengeful Hatfields to rescue him." Shelby pushed himself away from the table and stood. "Thanks for the hospitality, but I gotta go now."

"Now you just hold on there a second, Shelby Hatfield," Sally interjected. "You cain't just amble off and leave me hanging too, wondering how it all ended." She sat with a thump, not allowing him to leave.

Shelby laughed, "I didn't mean for it to sound that way. Let's see. The hanging ended the way they all do. Cottontop took a short drop into eternity. But folks was so worked up about it all that when the trapdoor beneath that poor man's feet opened and nobody rode to the rescue they left feeling cheated." And so November passed into December.

One crisp December morning when the white sky hinted of snow, See Bird hitched up the mare to the wagon and brought it round to the front of the house. "Hurry up, gals. Climb aboard. It's a gettin' cold up here."

"Keep your powder dry, See Bird," Sally snapped. "I had to get the stone hot so's Gertrude and me wouldn't freeze. There now, honey," she said in a gentler tone as she handed up her daughter and followed her onto the seat. "You just scrunch in there between your Pap and me. I'll wrap us up in this big old blanket with the hot stone in it, and we'll be as snug as a bug in a rug." Gertrude beamed, her rosy face alight with the excitement of going to town.

See Bird flicked the reins. "Let's go Sooky," he said and the wagon headed off to the west, up and through the low gap in the ridge and down the road toward Upland, several miles away. Nearly two hours later as they rounded a bend the clean, white spire of the Hardshell Baptist Church came into view on a small barren rise. Its cemetery spilled down the hillside behind it. The several buildings that comprised the hamlet lay scattered about the glen with little sense of planning. Beyond the church were a few houses, one with a faded picket fence, and then the downtown proper – a small clapboard building that served as a boarding house and hotel, with a café on the first floor. Then there was the general goods store, the town bakery, and the local bank – all on the same side of the street. Across from them was the blacksmith and livery with the corrals out back. And just past that, across from the bank stood the notorious jail which Cap had exited so precipitously, now sporting a new brick wall. The final building at the end of the street, the school, now stood closed and shuttered until the summer session would start up again. Built by the Hatfields nearly twenty years before, the school boasted the same teacher now as then, Joe Butters, as strong a Hatfield partisan as lived in the area. He boasted that he had been shot once every year for seventeen years and could be picked out in a crowd by his habit of suddenly jerking his head to the side, as if to catch someone sneaking up on him. See Bird and Sally had determined that when Gertrude reached the proper age, she would attend here, as much for her need to socialize with other children as for the quality of education old Joe could provide.

The clouds seemed to have lifted a bit as See Bird drew the wagon up before the general goods store and as he broke some skim ice in the watering trough for Sooky, he looked up and down the street for a moment. A few residents braved the cold as they hustled from building to building. The only manmade sound to compete with the whistling wind was the clang of metal on metal coming from the blacksmith. *I should really stop over there*, See Bird thought. *That fellow might have an extra pump bellows he'd let me have for cheap.* Then he turned to enter the general store following Sally and Gertrude.

A dozen different scents washed over him, from leather and denim to nails and soap. Gertrude rushed over to a bin of small objects and proceeded to unload them on the floor and play with them while Sally gravitated to the bolts of cloth. She bypassed the silky, more feminine materials with a lingering touch and studied over the floral and paisley designs on the linens and calicos. See Bird wandered over to the glass-topped counter, behind which stood a robust-looking man perhaps ten years older than himself, his long black hair swept neatly straight back from his face so it rested just outside his collar. "Howdy, neighbor," he welcomed See Bird with a nod. "Anything I can do for you today?"

"Yessir, I do believe so. We need some supplies. You can load them in the wagon out front." He dug out the list Sally and he had drawn up before leaving and handed it over to the clerk who studied it momentarily.

"I'll get right on this," he said with a smile. "You and your missus make yourselves at home, look around."

"Oh," See Bird said in a lower voice, "and one more thing. Could you get me a dozen of them gum drops, some of those horehounds, and a couple licorice wands along with a half-dozen peppermint sticks." He looked over his shoulder to be sure Sally and Gertrude were not listening. "Christmas and all – you know."

"Oh, yes. I know all right," the smiling man responded in a conspiratorial tone and a wink. "I'll pack them separately for you. Say, ain't you that Red Carpenter, what busted up that Kentucky posse a while back?"

"I guess so," See Bird answered.

"Well, this is my lucky day. I'm Hezicar Carter, owner of this establishment. Folks around here really appreciate what you did, probably saved a few good men's lives. Cap couldn't stop talking about you."

"Well then, I reckon it's a good thing he's gone." He chuckled, somewhat embarrassed.

"Ain't that a fact? Him sitting over in that jail holding court, why he had this town prêt-near turned into a circus. Like I said, pull up a stool over there by the stove and have a pickle and some crackers. You must be near froze. I'll get this stuff loaded right up for you. Oh," he added in parting, "and don't you worry about those sweets. They're on the house. Least I can do. Russell," he called to a lanky boy about twelve years of age who was stacking some canned goods on a shelf, "That's my oldest son," he said to See Bird, "Come here boy. Take this list and load it on the wagon out front. I'll tally it up." And off he walked toward the candy counter, humming some nameless tune, as his son went about his task.

"Bird, come here a minute. I want to show you something," Sally called from across the store. She was standing by a rack of factory made men's suits and shoes. "Now wouldn't you look just grand in an outfit like this?" She held up a yellow men's suit coat over a white shirt with a stiff collar for him to admire.

Getting into the spirit of the moment, See Bird pretended to seriously consider the outfit, ignoring Sally's teasing eyes. "Yes, - as a matter of fact I like it. I don't have anything like it at home. It would make a hit at Christmas, goin' to church and visiting with your relatives – that's for sure, darlin'." He felt the material of the sleeve as if he were evaluating it.

Sally started to pull it away, uncertainty replacing mischief in her eyes. "Oh, Bird, I was just teasing," she said but he held onto the sleeve.

"Really, Sally," he said, "I kind of like it. And these shiny yellow shoes would be just the thing to set it off."

Worry creased her brow as she pulled the sleeve from his grasp. "If you get this flatlander outfit, it for sure would set me off," she stated firmly.

See Bird could not conceal his mirth at her discomfort a moment longer and laughed aloud. "I'll tell you what. I'll buy this outfit if you go over there and buy one of those slinky dresses some of the girls are wearing these days." He pulled her close, discarding the suit. "But on the other hand, if you were to do that, Mrs. Carpenter, I'd never get my chores done outside, 'cause I'd never get out of bed."

Sally's dark brown eyes stared up at his. "I don't ever want you to, Bird. I never feel so safe and loved as when you're holding me under them blankets."

They were interrupted by the sound of the clerk clearing his voice. Beside him stood another man, puffing himself up to look as officious as possible. "Mister Carpenter," the clerk said, "I'd like to introduce you to the mayor of Upland, Virgil Howard."

The one designated as mayor extended his hand, "How do you do, Mister Carpenter? Yes well, mighty fine to meet you and all." He hesitated, then barreled straight ahead, "Dangnab it, I might as well go ahead and say what's on my mind." And then he stopped again.

"Yessir, Mr. Mayor," See Bird encouraged, "that's probably a good idea. And I'd appreciate if you men would just call me Red."

"Thank you, Red." He rubbed his hands together nervously and started over. "A few of us men were talking the other night, over in my office above the bank – about Upland – and the area. Times are changing and we have to change with them. We certainly don't want to be left behind. Do we, Hezicar?" He paused, glancing at the clerk as if hoping he would pick up the conversation. Hezicar held his tongue but raised his eyebrows meaningfully. The two men stood there looking at each other.

"Mr. Mayor," See Bird interjected, becoming visibly impatient with the man's inability to get to the subject, "things surely are changing – and maybe even your town. But what has that to do with me?"

"You're absolutely right, mister – I mean Red. What it has to do with you is this." He rubbed his hands vigorously and then began again, "What it all boils down to is this – we have an idea that will put Upland on the map, and you're part of it, my friend. We have done a bit of checking around, ah, the wonders of modern telegraph. And did you know that Huntington this very year is getting telephone service?"

"As you were saying, Mr. Mayor?" the clerk interrupted, trying to bring the wandering politician back to the subject.

"Yes, as I was saying" - then grasping the thread again, "Yes, we want you to be a part of it. Actually, we want you to be a big part of it. There is no doubt you are a great horseman. It seems you've ridden extensively in what people are starting to call the rodeo circuit out west. And the word is out, young man," he wagged his finger in See Bird's baffled face, "the word is indeed out that you can twirl a lasso, or whatever the danged thing is called, with the best of them. The boys still talk about how you roped both those men with one lasso – is that right?"

See Bird held up one hand as if to block the flood of words. "Please, sir. What you're saying kind of makes some sense, but unless you can rope me in, I got business to attend to before we head home."

"Dangnab it, Red. Ain't you listening?" the flustered mayor seemed ready to explode. "We want you to star in our own Upland rodeo next summer, the first ever. Not the first ever rodeo, of course – the first ever rodeo in Upland. There, that says it all. Oh, and one more thing. We'll pay you, too."

Huge, heavy flakes of snow, driven by strong northwesterly winds hurried the small family and the heavily laden wagon on their homeward journey. Little was spoken, due as much to the elements as to anything else. Sucking on a peppermint stick, wrapped in a warm blanket, and huddled between her parents, Gertrude rode quietly as well, content to relive the excitement of her visit to town. Following their interview with the mayor, as soon as their goods were loaded, the family had walked over to the café where Sally had the distinct pleasure of eating food that someone other than herself had prepared. They spoke of the weather, of shopping and the food, but somehow the topic of the Upland rodeo was never broached. Sally felt that it was something See Bird had to work out for himself, and See Bird, in such pleasant circumstances, did not wish to introduce a subject which might cause a rift with Sally. However, after the supplies were unloaded and Gertrude tucked into her bed, Sally perked a pot of coffee and brought a cup for See Bird and one for herself to the table.

"Bird, it's been quite a day," she sighed as she sat down across from him. "Tell me what you're thinking about."

See Bird eyed Sally, taken again by feelings of warm affection. Though at the end of a very strenuous day, her eyes sparkled with good humor as she sat back and shoved those wayward strands of hair behind her ears. He smiled. "Sally, I don't quite know what to think. At first I thought those two were crazy to think anyone here would be interested in a rodeo, and I'd hate to take their money only to have no one show up. And it can't be just a one man show. If something happened to me, like was I to fall off a horse and break my leg or something, what would become of their rodeo? So my first thought was to say no."

"But that wasn't your final thought, was it?"

"No it wasn't. I pondered over it a bit and got to thinking how much fun it would be. I got to be honest with you, girl. I love you and Gertrude and my life here, but I'd be lying if I told you that sometimes I didn't miss just saddling up Kiamichi and riding as far as I can see, just to find out what's there. And when I think of sitting on his back behind the gate in the arena, with all those folks hollering to see us ride, and then it flies open and that big horse digs in and shoots out to race around those barrels, cutting so close my leg brushes them, and the time is hollered as we shoot back, and everyone roars again," he paused for breath in his excitement, "well, gal, I mean to tell you there ain't nothing quite like it in the world – 'cepting sometimes when we're together."

Sally leaned forward, cradling her coffee cup. See Bird hadn't touched his. "Well, at least I know I rate nearly as good as a horse ride," she added with a gentle smile. Seeing his uncertainty she continued. "See Bird, I want you to know one thing about me. I ain't never wanted to chain you down, and I ain't never gonna. While I may have some questions about you killing yourself for the fun of riding, at the same time, honey, if that's what you gotta do, then do it better than anyone ever done it before." See Bird's shoulders visibly relaxed and he reached for his coffee. "But you're right about one thing," she said gently as she reached over to touch his hand. "Those old boys got their work cut out for them, if they think they can find anyone can outride you."

See Bird covered her hand with his and nodded. No other words needed to be spoken.

10

The Christmas Eve service at the Upland Hardshell Baptist Church was packed, so that even with just the four Advent candles lit, the small room seemed uncommonly stuffy. See Bird, Sally and Gertrude found space in a pew and along with nearly everybody else in town joined in listening to the Christmas readings and singing of familiar carols. To keep Gertrude's fingers busy and thus ward off potential trouble, Sally had brought along some of the little girl's knitting. There she sat, fingers working the needles quietly throughout the service. Sally beamed with pride, especially when a little boy two pews behind them had to be hauled out by his suspenders by his flustered father for crawling about under the pews, disrupting his neighbors.

Following the service, members of the congregation stood about, talking and swapping stories in small groups while the church ladies set up a punch bowl of hot cinnamon cider. The mayor and a number of other men gathered around See Bird, discussing, among other things, the "Upland Spring Roundup," as they had officially named their rodeo.

It seemed as though See Bird was not the only cowboy living in the tri-state area comprising that corner of West Virginia, Kentucky and Ohio. The town leaders had, in the mayor's words, "cast their breads upon the waters," not knowing what would happen, but they had been quite pleased with the responses received so far. Although only a few men had definitely committed themselves to compete, they had fielded a dozen requests for more information already. "Yes -siree –Bob," the mayor concluded. "It looks like we're going to have us a grand old time. Two of the entrants say they will attend because they have either seen you or heard of your reputation, Red."

See Bird smiled, pleased at the responses as well. He too had been concerned that the whole thing would fizzle out for lack of interest. He added, "Just one thing concerns me, Mr. Mayor."

"And what is that, my man?"

"I surely do hope you've got enough money to make it worthwhile for men to come all this way. I've ridden out West. These men do dangerous work, and they don't do it for free."

"Yes, well, ahem, I see what you mean, Red. We may need to limit the number of entrants. And there is the admission fee for all spectators. Still…"

"Maybe," the General Store owner said, "we could get the businessmen of the area to chip in some. After all, we are the ones who stand to gain the most from all those visitors."

The mayor beamed, "A prime idea, my friend – a capital one in fact." And so he continued. But See Bird had stopped listening. Across the room he watched as two little ladies dressed in black stood talking with Sally. Although he could not hear what was being said, See Bird could tell by reading Sally's body language that she was becoming increasingly upset. Now she folded her arms and moved one foot back as if to give herself more room for a fight. See Bird excused himself from the men and quickly walked to his wife's side.

"It just strikes us as improper," one of the ladies scolded, "that you would allow such a behavior in church."

Seeing Sally about to reply with words perhaps even less appropriate than whatever it was that upset the two wizened women, See Bird jumped in. "Excuse me, ma'am, but what behavior are you talking about?"

"Why, didn't you see?" the other one asked. "That child of hers was knitting throughout the whole service. It was quite disrespectful and should have been stopped immediately."

"And this is woman's business," the first one chimed in. "We don't need some ruffian to give us advice."

See Bird flushed and stopped smiling. "Ladies," he said, "That child of hers is also my child and she has a name, Gertrude. If you had taken the time to speak to her, she most likely would be able to tell you what chapter and verse the preacher was quoting. I don't mind what you just called me, 'cause I know the truth of it," he felt his anger rising as his voice lowered. Sensing movement at his elbow, he glanced to see Sally, a tight smile on her face, locking eyes with him as she rested her hand on his forearm. In a more controlled manner he finished, "My family IS my business. I mind it, and from here on in, I suggest that you mind your own." He turned away from their horrified gasps and ushered Sally across the room to where Gertrude and several other little children were sitting on the floor talking and tapping toes.

Both parents took the scene in approvingly. Sally spoke, "It's time to go, honey. Sooky is waiting in the cold, and we've a long way to go."

Gertrude jumped to her feet. "These are my new friends, Carrie and Charlie Carter. Bye," she waved as Sally handed her into her coat. "I'll see you again sometime." Her new friends waved and walked away.

"Honestly, Bird," Sally said as they moved toward the door, "I thought for a minute there you were going to say something rude to those two biddies. It's a good thing I was there."

11

Spring came to the mountains as it always does, slowly and in fits and starts. Like a flower, spring unfolded almost lazily, from the mountain trillium to the redbud and wood violets. The bear groggily emerged from his den and the woodpecker's hammering echoed again throughout the leafless forests. The pace of life quickened as the days lengthened. The April rains turned the roads into muddy tracks, and once again Sally had to exercise vigilance to keep the dreaded red clay at bay from the interior of her house. She laid out a plan for an extended house garden to supply most of their basic vegetable and herbal needs, and See Bird plowed the ground for it along with six acres for corn and oats to feed the animals and another two acres for tobacco, their only cash crop. One of life's treats for Sally and Gertrude came after supper, when See Bird would pick up his lariat and practice rope tricks. Gertrude never tired of watching her Pap jump through the loop as it swung side to side. At other times he would saddle up Kiamichi and run the sturdy mount through its drills. But these demonstrations were not for show. See Bird was well aware the cowboys who signed to participate in the rapidly approaching Upland Spring Roundup would have an advantage over him of actually having ridden and worked rodeos and roundups while he had been planting his fields. He worked to hone and maintain skills which, though unusual for a farmer, were the stuff of daily life for the westerner.

One afternoon, as he stood, practicing lasso variations on Sooky as Gertrude rode her past at a slow walk, a stranger surprised him. So intent was he on his rope work that See Bird didn't notice him until Gertrude stopped Sooky and pointed. See Bird turned and saw the man behind him.

"Excuse me, mister," the stranger said, "but I was enjoying the show so much I didn't want to interrupt. My name's Butler." The two shook hands and he continued. "I'm a reporter for the New York World newspaper, and I would very much like to do a story on this feud between the Hatfields and McCoys."

"It seems to me," See Bird said, "there's been too many of those stories already. They just seem to stir things up. Besides, I'm not from these parts, not a member of either family. Name's Red Carpenter."

Butler smiled. "I'm well aware of who you are. The good folks in Upland told me about your exploits and directed my feet in this direction, as you are on the path to the man I wish to interview, one Devil Anse Hatfield, and could perhaps direct me further."

See Bird paused thoughtfully. "I am not sure you want to do that, Mr. Butler. Devil Anse is a mite suspicious of strangers and believes no newspaper has yet done fair by him."

"And that is exactly my point. All my colleagues sit down there in Pikeville, scribbling down whatever the McCoys tell them. Just the other day Randolf McCoy made two New York papers by saying he knows for sure there is a heaven because he has lived next to the devil for years. Now your governors and courts are in the act. Why, this situation has even been heard by the highest court in the land. Someone, it seems, should tell the other side of the story. What do you say? Will you help me?"

See Bird studied the man before him. He looked harmless enough. He had no horse, carried no visible weapon, and besides a shoulder bag that looked stuffed with papers and some food, carried nothing that would seem to threaten anyone. The citified little derby crowning his head helped See Bird reach a quick decision.

"I'll tell you what I will do for you, Mr. Butler. I'll walk you to the right trail and point you in the right direction. Devil Anse's place ain't all that far from here. My advice is to not look like you're sneaking up on him 'cause you'll for sure be spotted before you get there anyways. Deal honestly and openly with the man and you'll have nothing to fear." The reporter nodded, looking both worried and excited at the same time. See Bird escorted him to the road that led up to Island Creek, gave him directions and bade him goodbye. Then he turned back to the house.

"Who was that?" Sally wanted to know when he reached the porch.

"I'm not sure," See Bird said. "The man said he was some New York reporter trying to set the record straight. Seemed harmless enough. I don't know though. Anyhow, I don't reckon he'll cause Devil Anse to lose much sleep. I'm sure we'll hear about it later."

As things would have it, the next evening, directly following supper, Shelby Hatfield rode by and dismounted at the front porch, calling out for See Bird. Rising from the table he sauntered over to the door to greet Shelby, standing by his horse, wearing a huge grin.

"What's all the ruckus about, Shelby? Come on in for a cup of coffee. We're just finishing up in here."

"I'd love to, Red, but I got to get me over to Upland and send a wire off to Logan, care of Devil Anse. I just thought you might appreciate the news."

"I might at that. And what might the news be?"

Shelby chuckled to himself as he lined up his thoughts. "Red, do you recollect a stranger under a little derby passing through yesterday?"

"I sure enough do, old son. Claimed he was a New York reporter named Butler."

"Ha!" Shelby laughed. "He warn't no reporter, and he warn't no Butler either. Devil Anse got wind of a bounty hunter named Baldwin who was going to disguise hisself and capture Devil Anse all by his lonesome. The fool was bragging on it down in Pikeville."

"What happened to the man? He seemed harmless enough to me," See Bird asked.

"I guess he was, at that. Devil Anse played along with him, acted flattered, showed him around, and never gave him a chance to draw down on him. Last night he tucked Baldwin in nice as you could wish. Then this morning bright and early, about 4 AM, Devil Anse called him by name for breakfast. That man nearly jumped out of his skin when he was called out. The game was fairly up and he knew it. The poor boy was shaking so hard he could scarcely touch his biscuits and gravy. But Devil Anse talked to him as nice as to company. And afterwards he walked the stupid hawkshaw over to the ridgeline, pointed the way towards Logan and sent him hurrying on his way, minus his sachel. He told Baldwin he'd better hurry up 'cause there's some mean old boys around who would not treat him nearly so hospitably."

Shelby shook his head in mirth. See Bird just smiled at Devil Anse's sense of humor.

"And you want to hear the corker? At the bottom of that bag of his was a teensy lady's gun what held all of two bullets – a Derringer it's called." He looked at See Bird in disbelief. "Now don't that beat all?"

"There's no accounting for some people's thinking, if you can call it that," he responded.

"You sure you don't want to come on in for a few minutes?" Sally asked from beside See Bird.

"I'd like to, Sal. I really would, but I gotta get goin'." He remounted his horse and turned it toward Upland. "I just thought you folks might get a kick out of the news." And he rode away.

As the two turned to reenter the house See Bird said thoughtfully, "I'm going to have to be more careful than ever. This turned out all right, funny even, but it shows those bounty hunters are not giving up, and more folks are liable to get hurt before this is all done." Then, retrieving his lasso from the porch swing, he shook it out and smiled in her direction. "Say, gal, I've been working on a double loop lasso stunt, and I think it's about ready for the paying public. Let me show you how it's done before we turn in tonight."

12

The day dawned bright and clear for the first ever Upland Spring Roundup, as it was officially designated. The family rode in early in the morning, Sally and an excited Gertrude in the wagon drawn by Sooky, while See Bird walked Kiamichi behind. In the bed of the wagon were his war-bag full of riding gear, a basket with plenty of food, and soft blankets with a large parasol Sally kept for just such a special occasion. The town fathers had clearly done their homework in preparation. Someone even hung a huge welcoming banner across the main street between the dry-goods store and the blacksmith's. To See Bird's trained eye, it appeared there were very few slip-ups. One noticeable shortcoming was in the housing area. Not enough thought had been given to where the crowds of people, should they arrive, would spend the night. Upland's small boarding house and café was not nearly adequate to accommodate all the visitors who arrived the day before. After brief consultations, the village trustees had thrown open the school house doors and provided whoever was willing to throw down on the hard floor a place to spend the night out of the chilly spring weather in comfortable warmth – firewood for the stove provided free of charge. The offer was taken up by many, used to sleeping conditions not much better at home. Soon a carnival atmosphere emerged as strangers became friends and old friends spent hours exchanging news and gossip.

Ma Evans and her two daughters did a booming business at the café, catering to so many customers they were forced to set up a schedule so that people could eat in shifts. Mercy and Sam, her two daughters did not mind working the long day at all. Constant business made the hours fly. Also, word seemed to have gone out that two attractive, friendly young women who knew how to cook also knew how to smile and laugh at bad jokes. Those customers would most likely have been quite surprised had they peeked into the kitchen. There, slaving over the hot stove and cutting board was neither Ma Evans nor either of her daughters, but Old Tony Evans, Ma's husband, the real power behind the throne. He discovered long before that business noticeably improved when he stayed out of sight. And while, if he thought on it much, it might have hurt his feelings, the jingle of those lovely copper, and even a few silver tips eased the pain considerably. Other local entrepreneurs set up food booths and the scent of hog roasting drifted tantalizingly on the light breeze.

However, not all the stomach's needs could be satisfied at Ma's Café and Boarding House or the food vendors. Although there were no bars or saloons in Upland there were already several stands set up to help quench the thirst for something stronger than Ma's coffee. Moonshine, though technically illegal, was smiled on, or at least ignored as a way for farmers to get their surplus corn to market. As long as the men could hold their liquor, all would be well. From past experience, though, See Bird was aware that as the day wore on into evening, and as the liquor flowed ever more freely, a fistfight or fights even rougher were likely to occur. The ladies and most "decent folks" avoided these areas. See Bird, an abstainer who tried getting drunk a number of years ago and found it made him sick, just glanced at them and went his way.

See Bird's attention was drawn to the center of the action – to the grandstand built directly behind the livery and blacksmith's shop. Constructed of fresh milled lumber, the sturdy structure could seat several hundred people in a horseshoe-type arrangement with the open side facing away from the blacksmith's. Two gates, one on either side, controlled admission while directly behind the blacksmith's were the corral and entry gates and chutes for riders and animals. As he studied it See Bird decided proudly the Upland Arena would rate favorably with almost any small venue of its type west of the Mississippi.

As the man with the most experience in this sort of undertaking, and as the headliner, was consulted on all ideas concerning the Upland Spring Roundup. He found the village fathers willing, even eager to learn how to conduct a rodeo. Mayor Virgil Howard, although seemingly unable to march a thought through a complete sentence in a straight line, proved himself an apt pupil. He would be one of the judges and the announcer. The owner of the dry-goods store, Hezicar Carter, and old Joe Butters, the schoolmaster, completed the judging team.

As the time for the start of the actual tournament approached, See Bird, carrying his war-bag, walked Sally and Gertrude toward the grandstand. People were already filing in through the two gates. Some of those inside were using the occasion to spread out their picnic lunches in the stands.

"Sally, I've got to go get dressed for this wing-ding," See Bird said as they were about to take their places in line. "It wouldn't do for me to enter in my farmer duds."

"That's fine, Bird," Sally said with a smile. "We'll be cheering for you, won't we, honey?"

"We surely will, Pap," the little girl answered, her face a picture of serious consideration. "Listen for me clapping."

See Bird lifted her up and planted a kiss on one cheek. "I'll count on it," he said and gently deposited her back on her feet. Sally looked indescribably fetching in her paisley patterned dress and matching sun bonnet. They smiled at each other and squeezed hands before parting. As he walked away he heard Sally admonishing the child.

"Honey, please put your bonnet back on. It's gonna be hot in there."

"But Ma," the child protested, "it makes my head feel all tight." He smiled and turned the doorknob, entering a small room under the stands.

"Ladies and gentlemen, may I have your attention, please." The mayor, speaking through a megaphone, quieted the assembled crowd. "Ahem, yes. Today, we present for your enjoyment the first ever, but we certainly hope it won't be the last, of course anything…"

"For Pete's sake, Virgil, go on," urged Hezicar at his elbow.

"I mean to say," the mayor picked up his train of thought, "rise and greet the modern gladiators, your heroes of the Upland Spring Roundup, the grandest show on dirt." He pivoted slightly to face Mr. Carter. "I kind of like that phrase 'The gr…'"

"Virgil, put the megaphone down when you're talking in my direction." The grocer reached for it and drew the mayor unceremoniously to his seat just as the gate directly below them opened and a cavalcade of mounted men, each carrying the banner of his home state, and riding two by two came prancing into and around the arena. The crowd rose to its feet and roared its approval. Cowboys from states as near as Kentucky and as far away as Texas rode proudly beneath their flags, twice around the ring and then out the same gate they entered. The gate remained open as the last rider departed.

When the crowd had quieted somewhat, the mayor rose again, megaphone in hand. With Hezicar Carter staring at him warily he announced, "And now, may I present our very own champion, Red Carpenter on Kiamichi." As planned upon hearing this introduction, See Bird made his grand entrance. Kiamichi, who had participated with See Bird in dozens of rodeos across the West before See Bird had taken residence here, knew how to make a grand entrance as well. Prancing as proudly as a Tennessee Walker, he high stepped into and around the arena, seeming to enjoy the adulation of the crowd. See Bird rode as he always rode, back straight, reins loosely held in one hand. With the other, he waved his traditional, uncreased, black-slouch hat with a single feather in its brim, symbolic of his Choctaw heritage. His tan linen shirt was offset by the brilliance of the scarlet bandana round his neck. Batwing "show" chaps with silver conchas and trimmings completed the outfit. But instead of exiting the arena, Kiamichi pranced to the center and reared on his hind legs while See Bird stood in the stirrups and waved all around, bringing the crowd once more to its feet.

"Ma! Ma! Look at Pap. Everybody's clapping for him. Isn't he grand?"

Sally wiped tears from her cheeks. She had never seen him like this. A quiet man who shunned attention, he now gloried in the spectacle he helped to create. "Oh, yes indeed, child. He is that for sure."

"But my Pap can't hear me or see me," Gertrude protested.

"He will, honey. You just keep waving."

See Bird was having a difficult time locating Sally and Gertrude in the seething mass. Suddenly, above all the noise, rose the call of the Whoop-or-Will, repeated over and over. Focusing on that, it took but seconds to find and identify Gertrude standing on the bench, waving, and beside her, with her fingers still in her mouth for one more call, stood Sally, waving her sunbonnet vigorously, her undone flaxen hair shining in the sun. He acknowledged them both and Kiamichi came to a standstill as if cut from stone. Not even his ears twitched.

See Bird reset his hat and removed the long coil of stiff rope that hung from the left side of the saddle horn. He shook out a small loop and started twirling it from the saddle. Rapidly the loop expanded and See Bird raised the still spinning rope over his head. Still the loop widened until it seemed he might run out of rope. Then, amazingly, the loop began a slow descent around both the man and his horse until it was barely six inches off the ground. However, instead of coming to rest there, almost magically it began to rise until it was shoulder height. The rope whistled around the horse's ears with no more affect than a mosquito. Up and down – the pattern repeated itself, a man on a horse inside forty feet of spinning rope. As the rope rose one last time, he flicked his wrist and it sailed off to one side, landing in the dirt. See Bird raised one leg and slid off the side of Kiamichi, doffing his hat, and bowed to the appreciative crowd.

He then recoiled the lariat and ran through a series of rope tricks – stunts, he called them. He started with the merry-go-round, a small loop in a flat spin parallel to the ground. From there he would pass the spinning rope under one leg to the other hand behind his back, and reaching behind him with the first hand retrieve the rope and bring it around to the front again.

One stunt followed another. Maybe it was the pageantry of the event, or his excitement at doing something he loved so much – whatever the reason, his performance that day in the center of the arena became a thing of agility, grace, and beauty. His hands flew like birds, never missing a grip. One rope became two spinning ropes, then back to one again, only this time it was spinning vertically to the ground and See Bird skipped, almost dancing back and forth through the loop.

Gertrude was beside herself with joy, laughing and clapping almost continuously. Sally stood and as the performance proceeded, became quieter as did the entire becalmed crowd. She had watched many an evening as he practiced his "stunts." But she never imagined it could look so beautiful.

Finally, at a signal from See Bird, the mayor rose once more. "And now ladies and gentlemen, for his grand finale, Red Carpenter, the West Virginia Whiz, will attempt that most difficult of all throws – to rope an onrushing horse in a figure eight toss." Immediately after this announcement, through the gate emerged a rider on horseback charging in See Bird's direction. See Bird picked up the rope, shook out a loop and began its spin. Inspiration striking him, he suddenly spun the loop vertically, skipped through it, skipped back and sent it off at the galloping horse. The rope twisted in air, creating two loops, one of which settled down over the horse's head while the other captured its legs as it skipped through. The rider drew his mount to a halt just beyond See Bird and grinned widely, waving to the crowd as See Bird retrieved his rope and strode to Kiamichi. Gliding into the saddle, he once again stood the gallant steed, tipped his hat to the crowd, and kicked into a sprint to the gate. Once through, he was surrounded by the cowboy competitors, congratulating him and slapping his back. They knew quality when they saw it.

The cowboy tournament then proceeded in what gradually became a recognized rodeo order. There were only five events: Bull riding, saddle bronc riding, bareback bronc riding, calf roping and barrel racing. In order to increase competition, it was agreed upon in advance that See Bird would enter no more than two of them. Afraid that if all he did was strut around and play with ropes, the folks might think him some sort of a dude, he decided to participate in the saddle bronc and the calf-roping competition.

The first event was the bull riding. In most of the rodeos in which See Bird had competed out West, the bull was a Brahma bull, a cross between the big sacred cow of India and the Texas longhorn. The good fathers of Upland, however, had either been unwilling or unable to acquire one. In their place were substituted the meanest bulls in the area, brought in by their proud owners the day before. The range of dispositions varied, but generally they looked to be big, strong, and ornery. Just to be sure they were all in a fighting mood, a big cowbell was tied under the bull's belly. The constant noise alone would usually set the beast's temper off.

The first up, Wiley Berger from Nebraska, drew Big Bob, a local favorite with a definite nasty streak.

Red, now changed from his show chaps into a working pair, stood along a crowded fence with one foot up on a rail. Most of the spectators had never seen this event, and See Bird knew something they did not. Although this was a timed event, only fifteen seconds, for the rider it could be the longest fifteen seconds of his life. See Bird was hoping they might shorten it maybe five more seconds more, as riders seldom were able to maintain their ride for the allotted time. And if he survived until the timer bell was rung, and even if he dismounted safely, that did not mean he would be out of danger. An angry bull could, and often did, charge the rider and try to gore him. And See Bird noted these bulls did not have their horns knobbed, as was frequently being done in other rodeos. So he stood there along the fence with several other cowboys, all ready to hurdle over it if necessary to distract the animal and buy enough time for the rider to escape.

On the signal, Big Bob exploded from the chute, Wiley clinging to the rope loosely tied around the bull's middle with one hand, his spurs "scratching" continually at the animal's flank. The fearsome black bull spun continually, leaping and turning in mid air, then crashing back to earth. Wiley had a reputation for bull riding that was well earned, but after only a few seconds it was obvious the bull was going to win this round. Wiley was unable to maintain his balance on the bucking, spinning brute and in barely half the time allotted he was turned completely sideways on the bull and after one more spinning crash, was himself sent crashing into the fence, beside which he lay dazed for a moment before struggling to his feet.

Big Bob looked primed for a fight and snorting, glared about him, trying to identify the agent of his discomfort. Clearly, he felt himself under no requirement to forgive and forget. The bull spied Wiley as the man was pushing himself up off all fours, but before Big Bob could bring his full attention to bear, a cowboy sitting the fence leaped into the arena, waving his hat and shouting. Big Bob stood for a moment, unsure which way to attack. Then the cowboy who leaped to Wiley's rescue did an amazing thing. He took a step toward the bull, turned his back, bent over, offering his backside, and flapped his hat. Meanwhile, hands from the top of the fence were pulling Wiley over to safety. Big Bob needed no more encouragement. He pawed the ground and charged. As soon as the unnamed cowboy saw Wiley was out of danger he stood and screamed, pretending panic, causing a cascade of laughter to fall from the stands. He sprinted the few steps between him and the fence and jumped up three rails, scarcely two seconds ahead of the bull, who ground to a halt, bellowing in rage. He turned back to the center of the arena, and seeing no other tormentors, calmed immediately. When the gate beneath the stands opened and he saw an avenue of escape, Big Bob turned and jogged out to the crowd's applause. Cyril Barnett, Big Bob's proud owner, clapped the loudest.

See Bird was glad he had not signed up for that event. But he did not stay to see the other riders try their luck with the bulls. The second event was the saddle bronc riding, and he was on the roster for that. As the local representative, he was to be first out of the chute. The horse he had drawn, Moondance, had a reputation as an unpredictable, unbreakable, mount that would occasionally toy with its rider, lulling him into complacency, only to rock him with a series of ferocious patternless bucks. Few riders had ever withstood the pounding for the allotted full minute. Even as See Bird mounted in the chute, Moondance tried to turn and bite him. There was a wild, nearly insane look in its eye, and the few sounds See Bird muttered as he wedged himself in seemed only to enrage the horse more.

When the chute opened Moondance plunged as nearly all broncs do and then boiled over. See Bird scratched him with his spurs as required, but this horse needed no encouragement. He was a true outlaw. The first two bucks were the worst, nearly dislodging See Bird and sending him daisy picking. He held on grimly and Moondance nearly went to his knees but then came up flying, landing in a "pile driver" on all fours, legs as stiff as steel poles. Another "pile driver," and as See Bird prepared himself for yet another repetition, Moondance changed the attack in mid air, twisting sharply into a "side winder." For the briefest of moments, See Bird thought he detected a glint of savage delight in the eye of the horse as he twisted in an attempt to swap ends.

See Bird knew he would get no points for style on this ride. It quickly became a battle for survival. All of the rules worked to the horse's advantage. The rider may not change hands on the rein – he is not even allowed to wrap the rein around his hand, or to try to pull the horse's head down. There must always be daylight showing between the rein and the horse's neck. Moondance seemed aware the game was rigged in his favor and sought mightily to use the rules to dislodge his hated burden.

In the grandstand, Gertrude stood mesmerized by the spectacle. The little girl never in her wildest nightmare dreamed a horse could be this wild or that her Pap would be on it. But hers were the only eyes in the family that watched the event. Sally sat with her head bent down, eyes tightly closed. Once she saw Moondance explode from the chute that was enough for her and more than enough.

Second after second ticked off, See Bird clinging and raking, Moondance growing increasingly frustrated and infuriated. Finally, the thin line between sanity and insanity was crossed. See Bird, for the first time, felt a wary fear. He knew this horse would kill him if it could. It sunfished once, raising its forelegs and leaping forward only to land with one shoulder much lower than the other. As it reared, looking as if it would try the same maneuver again, See Bird became aware of a change in the balance between the animal and himself. Moondance reared far too straight. The horse was trying to fool the rider into thinking it was going to repeat the same thing, but instead it intended to crash backwards and roll over the rider, crushing him beneath. With a split second to spare, See Bird slid out of the stirrup, disqualifying himself, and leaped to the side, not a moment too soon as Moondance came crashing onto its back. One thousand pounds of maddened horseflesh squirmed and screamed before lunging to its feet. See Bird unceremoniously scaled the nearest fence as Moondance, seemingly unaware he no longer carried him, continued his mad bucking until some cowboys managed to direct him from the arena. From the stands came a respectful round of applause and some cheering. Not all the spectators knew of the life and death struggle just waged in front of them. But everyone who was there respected the effort See Bird made. A cowboy pulled up beside See Bird at the fence and said, "That looked like thirty-eight seconds of hell. Tough luck you drew him."

See Bird shrugged. "Ain't a horse that can't be rode. Ain't a man that can't be throwed," was all he said. The cowboy nodded in grim agreement.

The following event was the bareback bronc riding. The rules for it are very similar to bull riding. With only a surcingle, a broad leather band with loops on it for the rider to grip, tied around the horse's belly, the cowboy has about as much chance for a long ride on a frenzied bronc as does a bull rider. The cowboy puts a premium on his dismount. He tries to land on both feet with his back to the bucking bronc. It may hurt if the horse connects with his backside but not nearly as much as would a pair of hooves to the face.

The next event See Bird competed in was the calf roping. He enjoyed this event because of the high level of teamwork required of the horse and rider. Kiamichi was not a typical cross-bred mustang, but a full-bred quarterhorse that See Bird himself tamed and eventually bought from the owner of the ranch he worked for down in Texas. Larger than most mustangs, Kiamichi tipped the scales at nearly fourteen hundred pounds, and See Bird liked to say that most of the extra weight was in his brain. He had instinctive cow sense and could work a herd with minimum guidance from See Bird. Calf roping was just an extension of what working cowboys did every day. See Bird's trust in Kiamichi was as total as the horse's trust in him. It had to be in order to win at this event.

What Kiamichi may have lost in speed over the last several years he more than made up for in his almost uncanny ability to read cattle, to anticipate which way the cow was headed before the animal itself knew and to get there first. To the uninitiated, roping calves, throwing them to the ground and tying their feet together may sound like an unfair event, but See Bird knew, given the rules, winning this event against an animal weighing some two hundred fifty pounds was no sure bet.

See Bird and Kiamichi were the final contestants. Kiamichi tensed. On the signal the gate flew open and the calf took off running, gaining a thirty foot lead. The big horse dug in and flew after it with See Bird seemingly gliding above it, the loop in the lariat already spinning over his head. Everything depended on the cast. As See Bird released the throw he already knew it would settle over the racing calf's head. As it did, Kiamichi performed his part flawlessly, coming to a gradual halt so as not to yank the calf off its feet. Such an act would cause a ten second penalty against the rider. See Bird looped the end of the rope around the saddle horn a couple times and raced down the rope to the calf. Kiamichi kept the line taut, backing a step or two if it became slack. With every second counting against him, See Bird "flanked' the calf, reaching over its back and under its belly, grabbing the legs closest to him. Moving with precision, he heaved the calf up and over on its back, its kicking legs directed away from his body. Some cowboys preferred to carry the piggin string in their belt. See Bird learned from hard experience this did not guarantee it would be there when he needed it so he, like many a veteran rider, carried it in his mouth. He yanked it out and like lightning wrapped it around three of the downed calf's feet and tied it in a square knot. This completed, he threw one hand in the air. Time was called and the judges quickly inspected the knot. Kiamichi continued to play his part, keeping the line around the calf's neck taut. Nineteen seconds – not a record but only a second longer than See Bird's best previous time. And it was the best time of the day by three full seconds.

As the results were announced, the stands erupted in cheers and applause. The timed results made no difference to See Bird's friends and neighbors. It only verified what they already knew. This man was good. But his victory was also a win for all the residents of the Upland area, common folks who didn't usually come out on top. And many a resident would leave the grandstand that day walking just a little bit straighter. "Yes," one would say, "that Red Carpenter was an outstanding horseman, and if only that crazy bronc had not flipped over, he probably would have won that event, too."

The rodeo's final event was the barrel racing. When See Bird first participated in such an event, years ago on the South Texas plains, it had been a quarter-mile race around a set of barrels. Now, it was standardized in a cloverleaf run, entirely within the confines of the arena. On the signal the gate swung open and the mounted cowboy would bolt out, looping around a barrel to one side, then across the arena and around another, then to the barrel at the top and back to the starting gate. It was timed, but speed was not the only thing that would win the event. Perhaps it was not even the most important thing. This event was designed to show off the agility of the horse, its ability to make razor sharp cuts and to fire away to the next target at full speed.

For this, a horse like Kiamichi was bred and born and won more than a few in his early years. See Bird ruefully figured that had he not chosen to compete in the saddle bronc busting, he and Kiamichi would have stood a better than fair chance of winning this event. But things were what they were. As Sally would say, "That's that, and that's all there is to it." Hearing her voice so clearly in his mind repeating one of her favorite sayings brought a smile to his face. He turned from the fence and walked up into the stands to watch the final events with her and his daughter.

Following the last event, See Bird excused himself for a minute and joined the other cowboys under the stands in the little office for the payout. Jests and good-natured ribbing were the order of the day. If there isn't an old saying there ought to be one to the effect "A cowboy and his money are soon parted." Many of these young men traveled a far piece to compete, and Upland intended to show them a good time for their efforts. A number of local beauties were seen strolling about town on the arms of swaggering young men in broad brimmed hats, and See Bird guessed that before the day was over, based on a few jealous stares cast by local swains, some fists would fly. He also knew most of the prize money would not leave the carnival Upland had become for the day.

The mayor could not have been happier. The Upland Spring Roundup surpassed his wildest expectations, and visions of reelection by a landslide filled his head. He chattered on aimlessly as the cowboys thanked him and received their money. As See Bird stepped forward, the mayor beamed. "And here he is, my good man, the man of the hour. And what a demonstration we were privileged to watch today. No, sir. Don't thank me. All of Upland is at your feet, or ought to be, except for a few malcontents who will never be satisfied, but then…" he shrugged and seemed to lose his train of thought. "But then…"

"That's okay, Mr. Mayor," See Bird injected. "It was a great show. You done your town proud." He stood smiling silently.

"Yes, well. Oh, certainly. You have come to claim your prize money." He counted up a stack of silver dollars. "I only wish it could be more. For headlining and for your win. Here you are, Mr. Carpenter. One hundred and ten silver dollars."

See Bird scooped the money into his saddle bags and, with a touch to the brim of his hat, turned to go.

"Oh, by the way," the mayor added, "there was a young cowboy asking for you earlier. Didn't get his name. Wasn't from these parts. Thought you might want to know."

Puzzled, See Bird paused for a moment. He had seen all the competitors and none of them had asked for him, so he wondered who it could be. Unable to make heads or tails of the mystery, he shrugged and left, meeting Sally and Gertrude outside.

Sally looked radiant. She was talking with Hezicar Carter, impeccably dressed in a white suit and waistcoat, his hat in his hand. When they saw See Bird approach, they turned toward him. Sally tucked a wayward lock of hair back under her bonnet and Hezicar smiled, extending his hand. "Here you are," the man said. "I was just telling your lovely wife how much I enjoyed your work. I do believe your daughter and my children are friends." Just then Carrie, Gertrude and Charlie skipped by. "We live right over there behind the store. We're close enough to Huntington for me to maintain contacts there, yet living here in Upland, we get to enjoy the beauty of the hills."

Gertrude tugged at See Bird's pant leg until he had to bend down. "Excuse me for a moment, Hezicar," he said as he squatted. "Yes, dear, what is it?"

Gertrude suddenly seemed nearly overwhelmed by shyness, but she spoke up without releasing her grip. "This is my friend, Charlie." See Bird noted the small freckled face child. "And that's his brother, Burgis. And this is Carrie. They have a baby brother named Everett, but he's too little to walk. This is my Pap," she said proudly to her new friends. “He’s the greatest cowboy in the world.” Pointing at a fourth boy who stood on the other side of his father, an older child, she added, “but I don’t know that boy.”

Hezicar laughed. “Yes, young lady, these are my four sons. The big boy’s Russell. And I’m glad Charlie is your friend. I’m also sure your ‘Pap’ is the greatest cowboy in the world.” Turning back to See Bird he added, “Well, I’ll be on my way. I have to admit I do not know much about rodeos and little Everett was ailing today so my wife stayed home with him, but my children and I thoroughly enjoyed ourselves and wanted to congratulate you. Good day to you folks.” With that, he turned and made his way up the street, Russell walking with dignity beside him, the others teasing and skipping behind.

See Bird took Gertrude’s hand on one side and Sally’s on the other and made their way towards Ma’s Café, winding through the crowd. “Sure are friendly folks around here,” he said.

“Honestly,” Sally said, “I barely laid eyes on that man before. He just walked up and started talking like we was family.”

“Sally, you’re so durn pretty that a man would be a fool not to want to talk to you.” See Bird then continued after a moment. “But that mayor of ours said there’s another man asking around for me, a cowboy, and I do not believe for a moment he had Mister Carter in mind. Well, darlin’, here we are.” They stepped through the open door into a room bustling with activity. Ma and her two girls were busily working tables, nearly all full. When See Bird was recognized, a chorus of congratulations and scattered applause filled the air. Ma brushed some sweaty hair off her face and beamed in his direction.

"Here you go, folks, right over here. We got us an empty table right by the winder." She ushered them to their seats.

"That pig you got roasting out back smells mighty fine, and I think I could most likely eat the whole thing myself. Why don't you just serve it up to us with whatever fixings you got to go with it."

"You got it, Red." With that Ma disappeared into the kitchen. Sally leaned forward. "Honey, you know we don't have to spend money here. I still got some sandwiches in the basket out in the wagon."

"Darlin'," See Bird answered, "I don't think I treat you often enough. Sit back and enjoy the hot meal. Besides, I made me a real killing today. In these saddle bags I got us one hundred ten dollars in silver. Plus, I sold three of those little Western carvings I whittled for five dollars a pop." He leaned back, cradling his hands behind his head. "I believe we can splurge just a bit."

The look on Sally's face told him they had company again. "Excuse me, See Bird," a man's voice said, "but…"

The speaker got no farther. A feeling like an electric jolt shot through See Bird, sending him to his feet so quickly he kicked his chair over.

"Luke Strebow!" he exclaimed. "I don't believe it." He shook the grinning man's hand so hard it almost looked like arm wrestling to Sally. But Luke shook it back just as hard. "Sally, I want you to meet my trail pardner from Texas days. Good Lord, man. I never expected this. Here, sit down." He made way for Luke to move in.

"Fine, See Bird, but I'm going to need two chairs. I want you to meet my wife, Mattie." From behind the big cowboy stepped a vision in black curls and blue jeans See Bird had nearly forgotten about. Mattie

O'Meara – the name conjured images of a time and place that seemed from another world.

"Mattie," was all he said before she wrapped him in a warm embrace. Sally seemed a bit nonplussed. Gertrude just stared.

He separated from her and turned to the table. "Mattie, this is my wife Sally and our child Gertrude."

"Red, or is it See Bird? I never know what to call you. I knew you as Red, but Luke here insists on calling you See Bird." Turning to the table, Mattie noticed Sally's discomfort at her open display of affection for her husband. "Sally, I hope we can be good friends," she said. "Red and me go back a ways is all. He saved my life once, and I'll never forget it. Now what are you folks having for dinner?"

13

Luke may have been just a tall, gangly kid when they had ridden the Chisholm Trail together, but See Bird had to admit the man had filled out considerably since. He didn't look soft by any stretch of the imagination, but clearly, someone had been feeding him well.

Mattie had grown up as well. No longer the flirtatious daughter of a roughhewn squatter, she had settled down. Though her physical attributes were as apparent as ever, there now was added a steadiness and sureness about her that bespoke a sense of responsibility and a willingness to stay at a task until it was finished. He wondered ruefully, as he studied the pair how he must have changed in their eyes. Luke was explaining how they learned where See Bird was: "We had to go into Rimes one day to pick up supplies and there was a flier for the Upland Spring Roundup. The title sounded a mite windy to me and I turned away, but Mattie here called me back to it. And sure enough, there was your name, big as life. I guess you could say we just took it as a sign and made arrangements to come east. I gotta admit, pardner, you got yourself tucked into some mighty imposing landscape here. Nothing like it back in our part of Texas. And how'd you manage a daughter who looks to be about five years old? You ain't been gone nearly that long."

See Bird filled Luke in on how his life had turned when he met Sally that day on the Huntington riverboat landing. He explained that her husband, a local law officer and father of Gertrude, had been killed trying to serve a warrant, and so he had stepped right into a readymade family. On hearing this, Luke nudged Mattie with his elbow to get her attention. She and Sally had been conversing in low tones. "Sweet lamb chops," he said to Mattie, "maybe you should be the one to give See Bird the news."

Mattie blushed and looked his way. "See Bird – Sally, Luke insisted I be the one to tell you. I am with child."

Sally gasped softly and smiled, reaching for Mattie's hand to give it a squeeze. It was clear the two were on their way to becoming fast friends. See Bird was speechless at first, then mustered his thoughts to some coherence. "And you folks came all this way. Well, it's for sure you'll be staying with us for a while. There ain't nothing else for it. I am so hornswoggled, Luke, Mattie, I don't think I can eat a bite."

"Well, if you don't, See Bird, we'll eat it all. We watched the entire rodeo," Mattie emphasized, "and we ain't had a bite to eat."

Later that evening, as they approached Warm Hollow via the familiar low gap in the west ridge, they paused a minute so See Bird and Sally could show Luke and Mattie the lay of the spread. "How absolutely lovely," Mattie sighed.

As the wagons rattled down to the house Luke commented, "It's obvious you built this place. You always were gifted with your hands." Catching Sally's quizzical glance his way he added, "You see, Sally, your husband didn't only save Mattie's life. I owe him mine as well."

"If you people don't mind," See Bird said, "I'm getting a bit wore out from all the goo. Sally, why don't you and Gertrude show Mattie around and freshen up a bit? I'll show Luke around out here. We'll be in directly."

"It appears to me," Luke observed wryly, "that no matter where you go, See Bird, you always manage to find the hot water." Placing his cup of coffee carefully on one of Sally's saucers, he continued, "The only difference I can see between then and now is that instead of facing down a gang of outlaws, you've got half the state of Kentucky up in arms. What do you plan on doing about it?"

See Bird raised his hands, palms open, in exasperation. "Blamed if I know, Luke. Cap's back in jail, got another year for another gun fight. Claimed self-defense, and that may be the truth of it. A fellow can get a mite skittish when folks are hunting his scalp. I'm just hoping that in time…" He let the sentence hang in the air unfinished and rested his hands on the table before him. He was about to continue when both men heard the sound of a horse approaching the house in a hurry.

Sally was already at the door as the two men rose from the breakfast table. Mattie was up in Gertrude's loft, listening as the child shared with her the important objects in her world. "Shelby Hatfield," Sally called, "What in blue blazes are you doing down here at this time of the day? Come on in and take a load off." She ushered the young man into the room. He stopped when he saw her company.

"I'm sorry," he said. "I don't mean to interrupt anything."

"That's okay," See Bird said as he walked up to Shelby. "These are friends from the old days, just come to town to see the rodeo and catch up on the news." He introduced Shelby to Luke and Mattie who called down from the loft, and then led him over to the table where they all sat down. Sally served coffee all around and took a seat as well. Seeing Shelby's reluctance to speak in front of Luke, See Bird reassured him, "It's okay to talk here, Shelby. Luke here and I go back too far to keep secrets from each other. Now what's going on that puts you in such a state?"

"Thanks, Sally." He took a cautious sip from the mug. "Umm. You sure know how to perk up the coffee." Then, deciding to take See Bird at his word, Shelby launched into his news. "Cap busted out again, and headed for the hills. Last time he did that the law just turned a blind eye." See Bird nodded. "This time though, Ran'l McCoy whipped together a huge posse to hunt him down once and for all. He even wore a squirrel tail tied to his cap like he was ol' Dan'l Boone or something. Well sir, as word got around a few more of the boys joined in with Cap, but there was so many hawkshaws with old man McCoy, they couldn't face them so Cap led them all back up the Tug Fork to Devil's Backbone."

Seeing the puzzlement on Luke's face, Shelby explained. "The Devil's Backbone is a place up the river where the rocks stick straight up in a row and the river narrows as it squeezes past. It makes for a natural fort. Word has it that back in the day, Devil Anse himself held off a whole company of Union soldiers from there by hisself. Some say as how that's how he got his name. Point is, it would be suicide for anyone to try to attack up there 'gainst men what are dug in.

"Anyway, Cap and some of the boys went to ground up there, one step ahead of McCoy's posse, and a helacious fight broke out. Pardon my French, ma'am, but it was so." He nodded toward Mattie who smiled in response. "Every time that Kentucky bunch worked up the nerve to attack, they was drove back down, and they was losing men. At the end of the first day Cap had two men hurt, but they had killed two of the posse and wounded another seven. On the second day the posse got reinforcements and everybody just hunkered down and let fly at anything that moved. On the third day someone got the bright idea to blow up the whole danged mountain with dynamite, Cap and the boys with it." He paused for a swallow of coffee.

Luke interjected with that disarming smile of his, "See Bird, that crew run by Slate out in Oklahoma cain't hold a candle to this bunch. So what happened?"

Shelby continued, "When Cap saw the barrel of dynamite lit, he and the boys came out and tried to surrender. But as soon as they exposed themselves they was shot at like rabbits, three men hit, so they dug back in. Then, WHAM, the dynamite blew up and half the Devil's Backbone slid into the river. It was the craziest thing. The danged stream actually turned around and flowed the other way. But when the posse stepped out after the explosion, Cap and the boys what were hid opened fire, and I got to say, a bunch fewer of those hawkshaws lived to run and hide again.

"Well sir, that done it. They brought up another barrel of dynamite and blew the rest of the Devil's Backbone down into the valley, figuring that would surely put an end to the fight and kill anybody what wasn't already dead. It was a fearsome sight. The smoke, dust and noise was so thick a man couldn't see his hand before his face. To my mind, they was all crazy to think that by blowing up such a gorgeous chunk of God's green earth, they could bring peace to it. Now the Devil's Backbone is just a blowed up mess of rocks and busted trees."

He paused again to drain his cup. "Sally," he said, "that is mighty fine coffee. I don't mind if you fetch me just one more cup full?"

"Shelby Hatfield," Sally responded sharply, "if you don't finish telling us this very second what happened to Cap and the boys I'll give you the whole durn pot, all at once." Luke and See Bird chuckled, but Sally rose headed back to the stove. Mattie, by now had descended the ladder and walked over to the table, the better to hear what all was being said.

When all were settled down again Cap resumed. "Like I was saying, the Kentucky gang blew the mountain up and when it all settled down, it got unearthly quiet. Didn't seem like anybody could have lived through such a thing. They all stepped out. I think they was stunned themselves at what they done and just wanted to look. They was just standing there looking, from what I heared, when their left flank was just ripped wide open. After the first blast, when Cap saw they was going to try the same trick again, he led the boys down the side away from the river. The second blast just gave them the cover they needed to come around from the side without being found out.

"And when Cap and the others opened up from the side, shooting and hollering like banshees, that bunch dropped like flies. Those who could, turned and ran for Kentucky. Ol' man McCoy even ran right out from under his hat, or so I heared. Cap got clean away again. Anyhow, that's about it. But that's about enough, I figure. The fat's in the fire for sure now. Devil Anse has called for another meeting to figure out what to do about it all. I was sent with a few others to call the neighborhood to rally up at his place tomorrow morning." Looking around the table he added, "You're welcome, too, folks, as Red's guests."

After Shelby rode off to alert others in the area of the proposed meeting, See Bird stood on the porch with Sally and Luke. "Don't this just beat all?" he asked to no one in particular. "If folks aren't real careful now they're liable to be soldier boys swarming these hills soon. I heard in town that Governor Wilson had called up the militia and Buckner over in Kentucky was doing the same. If cooler heads don't prevail, we're maybe facing a war between these two states. It'd be a crying shame if that was to happen."

Luke nodded soberly. "That's the way it sounds, for sure. But what can you do about it, See Bird? Looks like maybe this bronc just cain't be rode. And I appreciate the invite tomorrow. I'm sure you folks should go, but I think it better if Mattie and me just stay here and keep an eye on the place for you."

"That's probably a good idea, Luke. Sal and me should be back by early evening if we get a good start. We might even make better time if we was to leave the wagon and just ride up. Would you mind keeping an eye on Gertrude 'til we get back?"

The sound of squealing little-girl laughter interrupted them as the door flew open and Gertrude, her black curls flying, burst out and past them, a wild-eyed glee on her face. Right behind her dashed Mattie, arms outstretched. "Oh, I'm going to get you now, you little rascal. You can't escape your Aunt Mattie."

"Aunt Mattie?" both men chimed in unison as she raced by in pursuit of the fleeing, squealing child. "I guess that answers your question for you," said Luke. "Ever since she learned of her condition, Mattie's been head over heels in love with the idea of a child. I'm afraid it'll take a few more before she gets it out of her system, pardner."

See Bird smiled as the two disappeared around the corner of the garden. "I'm figuring that'll be just fine with you, too, Luke."

See Bird on Kiamichi and Sally on Sooky rode into Devil Anse's compound bright and early the next morning. A few of the nearer neighbors had already arrived. See Bird observed that whereas on his previous visit he felt that perhaps Devil Anse's fort may have been just a little bit unnecessary, he was forced to admit now, in the light of men who would use barrels of dynamite to blow up other men, perhaps Devil Anse understood things better than See Bird gave the man credit for.

Devil Anse himself stepped out to greet the arrivals and usher them inside the house, not the fort. The kitchen was separated from the parlor by a narrow hallway past the stairs that led to the bedrooms upstairs. Levicy seated See Bird and Sally in the parlor and excused herself. Devil Anse sat on a short stool.

"I'm glad you got here early, Red. I'm wanting to talk to you about something that may help put the nail in the coffin of this here feud before everybody else shows up."

"I appreciate the confidence, Devil Anse. But what can I do? It appears the solution might just be out of our grasp."

The patriarch furrowed his black brow and said, "You're right of course to wonder. I'm afraid that even now it may be too late to avoid more bloodshed, but I gotta try. We all got to try." He looked directly at See Bird and then Sally. "I'm having trouble sleeping, what with mobs of hawkshaws blowing up these hills. Cap's now lit out for parts west, and that's probably for the best. I was talking with Levicy, and we come up with an idea, the only idea that we think might have a prayer of success. It won't be easy, and I'll need your help. But if I'm right and this works the only gunfire folks will be hearing around here will be hunters – of wild game, not men." He paused to allow See Bird to comment.

"Devil Anse, you know if there is anything I can do to bring peace to these hills, I will. My own family had a narrow escape, and I don't think I could ever go through that again. I know I can't," he added more quietly. "So what is your plan?"

The older man leaned back and See Bird thought he detected a weariness in him he had never seen before. Obviously, the situation was worrying him even more than he admitted. Devil Anse gathered himself and continued. "Here it is then. While we sit up here, looking for places to hide, avoiding those people, McCoy sits down there in Pikeville, holding court with the newspapers and anyone else who he can get to hear him out. He paints himself as the victim, and we look like a bunch of apes worth only blowing up with dynamite. He and his attorneys won't be satisfied until we're all dead or crushed." Devil Anse rose in agitation and paced back and forth in the small room. He stopped by the window, was silent for a moment, and then turned to face his guests.

"I've got to turn myself in. That's the only thing that will take the wind out of McCoy's sails. It's me him and his lawyer wants anyhow. With me out of the picture, he'll call off his dogs, I'm sure. Besides that, it'll give me the chance to testify, to tell my story and to show folks we ain't the monsters them damn papers been making us out to be. The main problem as I see it is to figure out how to surrender and live to see my day in court."

Worry filling her voice, Sally spoke, "But Uncle Devil Anse, we tried that before. You'll never live to get to Pikeville. Or if you do, they'll try to kill you there."

He smiled at his niece. "You're right, of course, if I was to go to Pikeville. But my warrants are from West Virginia. I just gotta get to Charleston in one piece. That's the other direction."

"True," See Bird added. "But that's still a mighty dangerous trip. Once the word's out what you're doing, and it will get out, that'll be the most dangerous hundred mile trip a man could make. You can't keep something like this a secret. The road will be swarming with men who'll want nothing better than to kill you for the bounty before you ever get there."

"You're right, too, Red. And I don't want to keep it secret. I intend to announce it publicly, to make a big splash about it. That's why I've got to make sure I do this right. Those papers have to see what kind of people we really are," he emphasized. Taking a seat again on the stool, he continued, "I've spoken with the mayor of Upland. He's notified the authorities in Huntington of my intents. I've been in touch with US Marshall Henry White. Technically, I will surrender to him and he will take me to Charleston. In reality, on the set day, I will go into Huntington, board a train with Marshall White and simply ride into Charleston to turn myself in. The authorities have agreed and in return will prosecute only for moonshining. "

"But..." Sally interrupted.

"But," Devil Anse continued, "I am not going alone. They have also agreed that in return for my voluntarily surrendering I may bring a small group of personal guards, all armed to the teeth, to escort me. But I am bound and determined that the men with me have to be men of judgment and character. They can't be hotheads who fly off the handle. They must look like just what we are, decent folks, but folks who will not be attacked with impunity. And they can't be all Hatfields. In a nutshell, Red, I am surrendering and I want you to be the lieutenant of my personal cadre. There's no one I trust more to help me pull this off. Will you do it?"

See Bird sat back stunned. He looked at Sally, who looked back at him and squeezed his hand. "You know, sir, that Sal and me got to hash this out. Last time I did something like this, it didn't turn out so fine. Give us a little time."

Devil Anse nodded his head solemnly. "That's all I ask. Let me know tomorrow, if you can. You don't need to stick around here if you feel you're needed elsewhere. I'll just rehash the plan out at the big meeting later, and speak privately to a few more good men, so's everybody knows what's going on."

Later, on the trail ride home See Bird and Sally were silent, their thoughts weighing all the implications of Devil Anse's desperate proposal. Just as they turned into the land leading to Warm Hollow See Bird looked at Sally, riding alongside and said simply, "I don't think I can do it."

"What do you mean, you can't do it?" Luke flared when he heard See Bird's response to Devil Anse's proposal. "You're the one who taught me, years ago, the difference between right and wrong, that right ain't just in the knowing, but in the doing. See Bird, if you turn this opportunity down because you're afraid for Sally and Gertrude, the next chance for peace in these hills may not come for years and until after many more good folks suffer and most likely die."

"I know what you're saying is true and all, Luke, but still when I think of the last time I went gallivanting off to help someone surrender, and all what happened..." See Bird shook his head as if to drive out the horrifying images, "I just don't think I could live with myself."

He looked so miserable standing there by the shed door, torn between his desire to end the bloodshed and his fear for the safety of his family. Luke's heart went out to his friend. He walked over to him and stood by him as See Bird stared at that blood-stained floor he had never been able to scrub clean and said more quietly, his arm over See Bird's slumping shoulders. "I can only imagine how you feel, what you must have to cope with. It must seem impossible. But you know what is right, and you will choose to do what is right in the end because you are that kind of man. I promise you this, my good friend, if you decide to go with Devil Anse, I swear before you and God that I will die before I let anything bad happen to your family. Mattie and me will stay here and keep watch over the farm. She loves Gertrude like she was her own girl, and Sally like she was the sister she never had. I love them both because you do. Look at me, See Bird."

See Bird tore his eyes from the stained wood planks and looked deep into Luke's. The Texan continued, "Once you reached inside me and pulled a bullet out and gave me a new chance at life. And then you did it again when you walked away from Mattie. Please, See Bird, I'm begging you, let me do this thing. There are no guarantees, I know, but just give me the chance to show my gratitude and try to pay down a debt I will never be able to pay off. Please. Let me help you. You don't have to carry the whole weight of the world alone."

See Bird searched Luke's pleading face for any sign of weakness or doubt. Finding only love and commitment, he finally let the merest hint of a smile etch his tight lips. "If that's the way it's gonna be," he said, gathering up his energy, "then, pardner, we've got a lot of work to do before I go."

14

Devil Anse may have been slow off the mark when it came to generating favorable publicity, but See Bird had to admit the man had pulled out all the stops on this occasion. It would have been a simple thing for his escort to pile in a couple wagons and ride into Huntington, board a train quietly and maybe sneak into Charleston. Instead, he had turned his surrender into a major show. The only thing See Bird could compare it to was the Upland rodeo of recent memory.

On the morning of the surrender, See Bird was waiting on the porch with Sally as Devil Anse rode in followed by seven mounted, grim-faced men, all heavily armed. Luke, Mattie, and Gertrude joined them when they heard the jingles, the creak of leather, and the blowing horses that announced their arrival. Devil Anse nodded at See Bird, who gave Sally a quick kiss and stepped into Kiamichi's stirrup, swinging astride. No sooner had he joined the group then Devil Anse swung around and led the troop at a fast walk toward the low cleft in the ridge that led to Upland.

Devil Anse set more than the pace; he also set the mood. The only sound was that made by nine men traveling quickly on horseback. Each one there knew what was at stake – nothing less than turning the tide of the conflict that tore at the heart of these hills. Each man there was personally involved. All had lost loved ones or friends. Most took up arms themselves fought to defend their homes and families. Several had been wounded in return.

See Bird glanced around and liked what he saw. In accordance with Devil Anse's instructions each man was either clean-shaven or had trimmed his beard or moustache neatly. All were dressed in the cleanest and best clothes they possessed. All were clear-eyed and stone-cold-sober. And all carried new Winchesters, revolvers, and knives. All but See Bird. The Winchester rode on the left-side scabbard and the big knife sat, as always, just behind his left hip, but he never felt comfortable or even particularly competent with a pistol. Perhaps what impressed See Bird the most about the men he would be traveling with was their sense of vigilance. Granted, this deep in Hatfield country it was not very likely that McCoy partisans or bounty hunters would show their faces, but none of these men had lived as long as they had by taking safety for granted. Eighteen flinty eyes continually scoured the landscape.

The band pulled up in front of the general store upon reaching Upland, and Hezicar Carter stepped out to greet them as they watered their horses and took drinks from their canteens.

"Good morning there, Mr. Hatfield, boys," he said. "Lem said he'd be right along. His little girl took sick last night, and he had to ride to get a doctor. Afraid he didn't get much sleep last night, but he swore he'd be here."

"Thank you, Hezicar. And please don't call me Mr. Hatfield. After all you folks have been put through, I wouldn't blame you for closing up shop in my face."

"Devil Anse," the shopkeeper looked flustered and embarrassed as he searched for the right words, "it's true things haven't been as smooth as I would have preferred, but I don't hold it against you. You're a man trying to do right by your family as you see it, and I'm of the thought that what you are trying here is the bravest thing I've seen done in these parts in many a year."

Carter was stopped by the insistent tugging at his elbow. "Pop," his tousled haired son asked, "can I go with them? I know most those men, and I can shoot a gun."

Carter looked at his son sympathetically. "Russell, you know there is no way I can let you go. These men have all been asked personally by Mr. Hatfield. I don't b..."

"Russ," Devil Anse interrupted as a new horseman reined abruptly to a stop, "I would love to have you as part of my escort. You'll be a fine man someday. But if things work out as I hope they will, this is going to be a very boring couple of days. I will be happy if I don't hear the sound of any gunfire. So you'll stay with your pop."

"Devil Anse, sorry I'm late but had some family business to take care of. I'm ready when you are." Lem Bocook, the late arrival, swung into line at the rear of the column reforming in the street, next to See Bird.

"Okay, men, we've got a train to catch. The Chesapeake and Ohio won't delay on account of a bunch of hillbillies lollygagging. They got a schedule to keep. Let's ride."

With the addition of Lemuel Bocook, the escort party was complete. A number of townsfolk stepped out to wave or just to stand and watch as the troop of mountain warriors rode down the main street and out of the hills and onto the floodplains framing the south bank of the Ohio River. But the hawkeyed men who rode with Devil Anse rode not to war, but to peace – at least they all fervently hoped so. And now the dangerous part of their journey began. They moved Devil Anse into the middle of the convoy and continued apace.

Huntington was a bustling city on the make. Electric lights had been introduced some five years before, and street cars clanged their warnings as they wended their ways along streets bustling with commerce. But the main feature of the city, the one in fact which created the city, was the extensive and sprawling rail yard for the Chesapeake and Ohio Railroad. From it were spinning off ever more lines snaking into the hills behind the city in an attempt to satiate America's ever-increasing appetite for the black minerals that lay beneath the wooded ranges. Devil Anse took in the scene and became even more convinced that this play of his had to succeed. He controlled hundreds and through his family, thousands of acres that could and should be developed to provide them with better lives. But as long as feuds and fighting continued, no coal companies wanted to place themselves or their employees at risk. So development lagged. As his horse stepped carefully across tracks toward the passenger and freight terminals, he swore that, come hell or high water, he would see this through to the end. His children and grandchildren deserved nothing less.

True to his word, US Marshall Henry White was there to meet him. In a businesslike but polite manner he greeted the famous, or as some would claim the infamous mountain man. "Well, Devil Anse, we finally meet. I'm United States Marshall Henry White, and I'm here as agreed upon by the authorities of the state of West Virginia and yourself to take you into custody and transport you to Charleston. Once there, you will have a chance to tell your story in a court of law." He scanned the horsemen. "Are these men your personal escorts?"

"That's right, Marshall. These two are my sons, Johnse and Robert E. Lee. The rest of these men are friends and neighbors who thought it would be a good day to take a train ride with me. I take it we have your agreement they may carry arms for their and my protection."

Marshall White looked uncomfortable but conceded the point. "That was part of the agreement as well." He turned so that as he spoke, he spoke to the gathered men as well as to Devil Anse. "As long as you exercise total control over these men and as long as they conduct themselves without blemish on the train, I have no objection to their traveling with you." Devil Anse's escort retrieved their weapons and saddlebags from their mounts as an attendant came to collect their horses for safekeeping until their return.

"All right then, men," Devil Anse addressed them at the side of the train. "Here we go. There are six cars on this train. I want Johnse and Robert E. Lee to ride in the engine. If somebody is foolish enough to try to commandeer this train you men will stop them. Other than that, do not interfere in any way with the operation of the locomotive. Two men will ride in each of the other cars, one to the front of the car, one to the rear. Stay alert for all who board at intermediate stops. We shall make a number of them, this train is no express, and trouble could come at any of them. Marshall White, Shelby and Red will ride with me in the final car. Maintain vigilance, but always mind your manners. We want to impress upon the citizens we meet that we are good men who deserve better than we have received."

Down the line the conductor's cry, "All aboard," rang out and the delegation from Logan County boarded the train without incident.

15

Marshall White settled in comfortably on the seat across the aisle from Devil Anse near the rear of the car as the powerful locomotive pulled away from the Huntington station, a large red brick building in keeping with C.P. Huntington's pretentions concerning the city bearing his name. Several dozen other passengers rode the train this day, but the word was out to avoid the last car. Only a well-dressed young couple recently married, and who undoubtedly had ears and eyes only for each other, had missed the warning. Having boarded the car in Lexington, Kentucky, they kept to themselves – the young man wearing a bowler and carrying an umbrella, one arm draped protectively around his bride's shoulders, whispering and pointing out the window at the beautiful full-summer scenery flowing by.

See Bird rode on the rear platform, enjoying this unique ride. In truth, West Virginia's natural beauty was on full display. To the train's left, the land was generally lower and gradually fell towards the big river. Homes and farms dotted the landscape. But to the right, on the south side of the train, the hills rose abruptly, towering over it and cloaking it in deep green shadows. The course was generally uphill as the rail line climbed from the river over low ranges into the Kanawha valley, wherein lay the capital city Charleston. So the progress of the train was slow and laborious. See Bird just thought of it as lazy and thoroughly enjoyable. He found himself wishing Sally were alongside him. She would so much enjoy the vistas unfolding around every turn.

Left to his thoughts, the time passed quickly. The first stop was in the small town of Barboursville, planted securely among low hills rising from the Ohio floodplain. See Bird peered around the corner of the car to inspect the platform and then stepped inside. As the train stopped, a few passengers disembarked, and about an equal number boarded, from appearance mostly businessmen and local merchants wielding carpet-bags bearing samples of their wares. One middle-aged man bearing such a bag climbed aboard the front of last car. Something about him caught See Bird's attention. The merchant was searching the car, not for a seat but for a person. His eyes scanned the car, noting and discounting the young couple, rapidly moving on, settling on Devil Anse, who was momentarily turned to look out the window, and on the man who sat across the aisle from him.

See Bird caught a quick flicker of recognition take place as the man battled for control of his face. For a moment, his blank mask lifted and See Bird saw in the steely glare a look of raw hatred before the mask descended once more. Instantly, the man excused himself and stepped back out of the car onto the platform and bent over his bag to open it.

Wasting not a moment, See Bird flew out the back door of the car and hurdled the railing onto the station platform, Winchester in hand. Raising his rifle, he barked, "Don't touch that, Mister! Stand up and step back easylike." In the next instant something with the force of a hammer knocked the gun from his hands. He dropped to a squat, trying to determine the location of the second shooter, whose lucky shot had found and shattered the stock of his rifle. Seeing See Bird disarmed, the shooter emerged from around the corner of the station, firing his revolver rapidly, buying time for his compatriot to dig the pistol from his carpet-bag. Bullets pinged and ricocheted off the coach behind him. He knew that given just a few moments more, Devil Anse's bodyguard would join the fray, but for him, disarmed and totally exposed, receiving deadly fire from two directions, in a few seconds it would be too late."

Instinctively his left hand reached for the Arkansas toothpick he carried behind his left hip. With a deft flick of his wrist and all the power his one hundred-forty pounds could put behind it, he hurled the big blade in the direction of the approaching gunman. Simultaneously, See Bird charged. The shooter wavered and fell forward as See Bird lunged for him, the big blade buried deep in his chest. See Bird wrenched the dying man's pistol from his hand before he even hit the floor. Even so, he felt a sharp stinging sensation crease the left side of his face. Rolling behind the corpse for whatever protection he could find, See Bird could hear the thud of bullets finding the man's inert body.

Finally the bark of a Winchester rang out over the noise of other gunfire. Shelby had now joined in the action from the train window. From behind the fallen body, See Bird saw yet a third attacker sprinting towards the platform from behind the station, beyond the rear of the train, firing toward the coach as he ran. The distinctive sound of Shelby's rifle rang again and the running man crumpled as if poleaxed.

The man who triggered the ambush saw his two partners in crime go down and realized his time was running out as well. His task was not to get caught up in a gunfight with guards but to get past them to the one he determined to kill in the first place. And that man was still on the train. The lone assailant leaped back onto the train as passengers ran screaming for whatever shelter they could find from the singing lead.

By now Devil Anse's other guards were streaming down the train toward the firing. See Bird lept to his feet and raised the pistol but dared not fire. The terrified visage of the young bride from the front row, pushed stumbling forward down the aisle toward Devil Anse, a helpless human shield. Noticing See Bird's hesitation, the man yanked the young woman closer to himself and glanced in See Bird's direction, favoring him with a triumphant smile. The smile froze on his face for eternity as the point of a sword drove through his neck. The hostage broke free and fled back into the car. The young bridegroom in the bowler appeared in the doorway and withdrew the point of his sword from the crimson bloom on the dying man's neck. Blood pooled and flowed out the door, running dark red onto the platform and dripping down onto the tracks.

The handsome young man smiled grimly at See Bird as he wiped the tip of his sword off on the dead man's shirt before retracting it into the umbrella sheath which hid it. "It appeared you men needed a bit of assistance. Cecilia and I are on our way from Lexington to the District of Columbia on our honeymoon. We were expecting an adventure," he said coolly. "I did not expect quite so much." See Bird looked down the aisle of the coach toward the rear of the train only to find himself staring down the barrels of two large revolvers.

Devil Anse and Marshall White carefully lowered the weapons and walked toward the front. See Bird stepped out of the coach and back onto the station platform. Shelby took up a position on the coach's rear platform, rifle at the ready. "You men," See Bird directed, "Make a quick search of the area and then reboard. Let's get this train moving as quickly as possible. Lem, tell the station master to fetch a doctor. I don't know if any of these bushwhackers are still alive, but if they are, maybe they can tell who put them up to this. Move fast. Think clearly." With that, he dismissed the men and turned to help Thomas Hastings remove the body of the dead attacker and place it on the platform beside that of the man See Bird had slain. He retrieved his knife, wiped the blade on the man's jacket, and resheathed it.

"You were quite handy with the blade, mister," Hasting said. "I thought they had you for a goner there."

"So did they. But thinking a thing is so, don't make it so," he responded as the two men walked back to step into the train coach.

The young man slid into the seat beside his bride who was bent forward, her head in her hands, sobbing quietly. "There now, darling," he whispered. "That animal is gone. He'll harm no one ever again. Shush now, my sweet Cecilia," he consoled as she collapsed into his arms.

Thank God Sally wasn't along, See Bird thought to himself. He walked back to where Devil Anse and the Marshall were seated. The train lurched, the whistle screamed several times, and the locomotive glided out of the station, picking up speed as it raced out of town and across the countryside.

"I must be losing my touch," Devil Anse said when

things had settled down a bit. "By the time I got my gun up and figured out who was who, it was all over. Never even got off one shot. But then," he said turning with a smile to the man next to him, "Neither did you, Marshall."

"What do you mean by that, you old sidewinder. I was on the wrong side of the train." He looked red with embarrassment. "Anyway, your men appeared to have things pretty well in hand." Looking at See Bird he added, "That was mighty quick thinking there, young man. I'm grateful to you."

See Bird nodded acknowledgment. "That's what I'm here for. If we have to fight to find peace, we'll fight. But there better be peace at the end of it all. Men's lives matter – even those men's back there. Now if you'll excuse me." He rose and slowly made his way to the front of the coach past the young couple and took up a position on the coach landing.

The remainder of the trip proved uneventful, which was just fine with everyone concerned. As the train jerked to a halt in the station at Charleston, they remained in the car while the rest of the passengers disembarked and the escort regrouped alongside Devil Anse's carriage. Finally See Bird, followed by Marshall White, then Devil Anse, emerged. The last off the train was Shelby. The men then stepped off to the rear of the platform where a trio of local officials moved forward to introduce themselves. Technically Devil Anse was thus transferred to the custody of the local officials and Henry White made his departure, shaking hands all around. In truth, Devil Anse was free to move about as he pleased, so long as he showed up the next day for his trial. Then the local officials themselves departed.

"Men," Devil Anse said, "I got us some rooms at the downtown hotel. This afternoon I have a meeting with my lawyer to work out our plan. I can't force you, but I really would appreciate it if you would sort of keep available, if you know what I mean. Can't tell who might be about. If newspapermen want to talk to you, feel free to tell them what you know, but watch your language. Remember, what you say will be read by women and children across the 'civilized' part of this country." The men laughed and swore as how Devil Anse could count on them. "And one more thing, boys," the patriarch added, if you travel about this our fair capital city, do so in pairs. Am I clear?" The men murmured their affirmation of the older man's instructions and he smiled at their open and honest faces, looking to him for leadership.

Later that afternoon See Bird was sitting in the overly ornately decorated lobby of the hotel, enjoying himself, watching the human traffic flow into and out of the building and along the busy street outside. Charleston was rapidly becoming the center for the new petrochemical industry, and new processing centers and factories seemed to be springing up daily. This town, he noted to himself, means 'business.' Lost in his thoughts, he was abruptly roused by the approach of Johnse Hatfield, the eldest son of Devil Anse. Smaller than the rest of his brothers, he also was better looking in that sense of the word women used. His reputation as a mountain Casanova was justly deserved. Even now his eyes scanned the lobby of the hotel prospecting for new conquests. "Man, Red," he said as he took a seat in an overstuffed chair, "I never seen the likes of it. This city's got the most beautiful girls I ever laid eyes on." See Bird just smiled. "But the worst of it is that I promised Pa I'd leave them alone, and it's killing me." Both men laughed at this admission. "Anyhow, Pa sent me down to give you this. He thought since you so carelessly lost your Winchester back there in Barboursville, he'd get you a new one," and he unwrapped the parcel he had set beside him.

See Bird received the new Winchester respectfully. He examined the weapon expertly, still shiny in its oily sheen, not because he was concerned about its condition, but to give himself time to consider his reply. See Bird was not a man used to receiving gifts, so he chose his words carefully. "That was mighty considerate of your pa, and I truly appreciate it. I respect the man, and each time I draw this weapon I'll consider the source. I expect it'll provide much game for our table." Johnse smiled appreciatively.

The trial the following morning was something of an anticlimax, trailing, as it did, the excitement of the journey. The courtroom was packed with newsmen and curious onlookers. Two rows were reserved for See Bird's armed guards, though on this occasion the weapons were left with attendants at the door. All the men were present, all sober, all well dressed and self-composed. The room was filled to capacity, but when Devil Anse was ushered in it seemed ready to burst at the seams. Though he stood barely six feet and weighed in at roughly one-eighty, he seemed larger than life. Space around him shrank and people moved aside. He certainly looked the part he played. Clad in blue denim pants tucked into his polished high boots, the faded blue shirt, and wearing a brown leather overcoat, he took the stand, crossed his legs comfortably, and testified to the charges against him with intelligence and a wary sense of humor.

Many a newsman, prepared for a confrontation with a surly, ignorant murderer was forced to rewrite his copy later that day. His dark eyes flashed flinty sparks only several times during the day's testimony, once when reference was made to the murder of his brother Ellison nearly ten years previously, the event which triggered the feud's explosion.

The distillation of whiskey had been going on for generations, long before it became a government controlled substance. Rural folks throughout the region had developed it as a way to sell their excess corn during a good year. Often the proceeds from the sale of whiskey were the only actual cash a farmer might see for a year. Nevertheless, the state was unable to prove its case against Devil Anse for the production and distribution of whiskey without paying the government required tax, and the federal case fell apart. As a result, after a one-day trial, he was declared not guilty and he strode from the courtroom a free man, rehabilitated, if not completely in the eyes of his fellow man, at least in the eyes of the law. All rewards and bounties leveled against him were removed, and it was a relieved and happy man who treated the friends and neighbors who had accompanied him on this dangerous journey to drinks and supper that night. It had been a canny move on his part to bring such men along. Devil Anse was now guaranteed that upon their return, word would spread quickly far and wide across the ridges and hollows of West Virginia and Kentucky of the court's resolve. From this date forward, any attempt on his life would be dealt with for what it was, attempted murder. For the McCoys and the lawyers and politicians who backed them, the writing was on the wall. Feuding days were numbered, and though memories are long in the forested hills from which these people sprang, never again would they erupt such murderous brutality.

See Bird meditated on the new state of affairs as the train back to Huntington chugged its way across bridged streams and valleys clothed in their full summer richness. *Next summer,* he thought, *Gertrude would be old enough to start attending school. Wouldn't that be something?* He recalled pleasantly his own years of school in the Presbyterian mission out in Oklahoma, and was pleased the Upland facility was a mere few miles from the farm. Sally and he talked about enrolling the bright little girl there, but with things so unsettled it did not seem all that likely it would be possible.

In the back of his mind a new thought emerged, one that had been nagging for him to deal with but so far he steadfastly ignored. The appearance of Luke and Mattie at the Upland rodeo caused it to flare anew. The truth of the matter was he missed the old ways, the days before the responsibility or family and farm, days when he would rise on the open prairie after a cold camp, and astride Kiamichi, head off for the next rodeo – maybe to Billings, Montana, or the grandest of them all – Cowboy Christmas in Denver. *Ah,* he thought as the train pulled into the Huntington Station, *those days are gone forever and I better forget about them. I got a family to attend to.*

16

See Bird's attempts to conceal his restlessness from Sally were doomed to failure from the start. At first, she thought it might have something to do with Luke or Mattie. But within a few days their visitors were off on their return west, and See Bird seemed, if anything even more unsettled than before. She was far too closely attuned to his moods to miss the signals he was unaware he was sending. And she was far too direct and honest a person to pretend or to allow him to continue pretending all was well. At first she was unsure what to make of it when he would rise abruptly from the porch and ride off on the big horse at a furious gallop, only to return a short time later and fold her passionately into his arms. Or when he would be working a new rope trick in the fading evening light and he would bring it indoors, shoving the table and chairs out of the way to provide space for him to work until blisters would appear on his hands in spite of the leather gloves he always wore when he worked the lariat. Gertrude would sit at the top of the ladder to her loft and watch her pap work until she could watch no longer and fall asleep, curled up in her bed while the lariat continued to whistle down below.

One evening, as the two of them sat on the porch at the end of another busy day, Sally confronted him directly. "Bird, something's been eating you since you came back from Charleston. I been hoping you'd work it out on your own, but it appears to me whatever it is has got you tied all up in a knot. We aren't going into the bedroom tonight until you tell me what it is." Taking a stab in the dark, she asked, "It ain't another woman, is it?"

She watched the pain course across his features, and for a moment her heart sank as she considered the devastation his answer could deliver. Her relief was palpable at his slow reply, "Honey, you know that can't never be the case. You and me finding each other the way we did was meant to be forever, and there ain't another female God ever created who could lock my heart in hers the way you have. I am ever grateful to know there will never be any other woman in my life."

"Then what is it, Bird?" She asked tenderly and reached for his hand in the fading light. "I'm right here—and always will be—for you."

Sally's words triggered a cascade of emotions in See Bird's soul. What he had always pictured there as an unbreakable interior wall that barred him from sharing his deepest dreams, hopes, and fears, tumbled and crashed in ruin. In this dream or vision a woman reached across the rubble to him, took his hand and drew him surely to herself. Wind swept the hair from her face and in the vast emptiness of time, he perceived it was the very woman sitting beside him on the front porch of the house he had built in Warm Hollow, his own Sally. But then, while an evening breath blew yet another lock out of place, the woman in his vision smiled at him, a hint of sadness in her eyes, released his hand, and with a faint nod of her head, turned her back and faced the other direction. He understood immediately what she was telling him, and awakening in this world he rose from his chair and knelt before the woman tied to him by destiny, and laid his head in her lap. Never again would he mistrust her love or her strength.

The following May, immediately upon the conclusion of the second annual Upland cowboy tournament, See Bird and Sally made their plans for the summer. One fine morning, as the whoop-or-will called from the edge of the woods, Shelby Hatfield rode in and as agreed upon, assumed immediate control of the farm chores. See Bird gathered his gear, saddled Kiamichi, and with final kisses for Gertrude and Sally, turned his steed and headed in the direction of the sunset. Sally and he had said their farewells the night before. In parting he hoisted Gertrude up onto the saddle and wallowed in the longest, fiercest hug of his life. He held it until the child broke it. "You come home to me, Pap, when you're done winning the rodeos. I'll still be here." Her lower lip began to quiver.

He kissed both her eyes and handed her back down to Sally. "Don't you worry your sweet mind about that, little one. You go to school and study hard. Learn your ABCs. I'll be back before you know it. Help your Uncle Shelby and Ma with the chores, and I'll bring you something pretty in the fall." Spinning Kiamichi, anxious to be started, in a complete circle he said to Sally, "I'll see you soon, gal, and I'll be bringing you something special, too," he said with a laugh.

Sally thought she had not heard him laugh so freely in ages and it made her heart sing, even in the sadness of their parting. "You just bring yourself home in one piece – and bring me a big wad of money. Now go!" she ordered and slapped Kiamichi's rump. As if released from chains, the eager horse leaped forward, heading for the familiar cleft in the low ridge. With a final high-pitched yell, See Bird reared Kiamichi, doffed his black slouch hat and waved it before disappearing from sight. Sally took Gertrude's hand in hers and said, "That's that, and that's all there is to it."

THE END

Epilogue

See Bird was a man of his word. One dusty August afternoon following a prolonged dry spell, Gertrude was overcome with joy to be met at the schoolhouse door by her pap, returning from his rodeoing out West. Once again, as had done months before, he swung the child up onto the saddle in front of him. But this time, as she rode before him, she did not stop chattering until he drew up at the porch step of their home in Warm Hollow.

Sally ran out to meet him. Handing Gertrude down to her, the tired cowboy slid smoothly out of the saddle and wrapped his wife in a long embrace, then turned to lead them back to the house. Sally looked up at him as if devouring his face. "Now let's see that big wad of money." And they laughed.

Afterword

One of the joys of writing historical fiction is the rewriting of actual history, changing dates or the chronology of events in order to enhance the drama. Sometimes the writer may even create events that never happened. "Devil's Backbone" is not history, though it is based on actual events and characters. Since the inspiration for this novel was Granny's 'recollections' to me as a young boy, I have no doubt that her Hatfield partisanship set the tone. I asked her once, when she was going on about Devil Anse, and what a fine man he was, whether the McCoy's had their own side to the story. She paused her rocking chair, took a long drag off her Pall Mall cigarette, stared straight ahead and ended the conversation by stating, "Yes they do – but them McCoys – they's stupid people."

I also remember asking Granny if she didn't miss See Bird when he would be gone so long. Every summer for years they would continue with what became a familiar routine, she holding down the home front while he went 'rodeoing,' and I could not conceive that she would have chosen such a life. "Didn't you love him?"

"Junior," she would say in a flinty tone, "don't you ever think we didn't love each other as much or more than folks who never let each other outta sight. But what kinda woman would I be to tie him to my apron strings?" She paused for a drag on her ubiquitous Pall Mall and continued in a softer voice. "I surely did love to see that man coming up the lane with his warbag in hand - and a big wad of rodeo money in his pocket." Then she would laugh. So, to a certain extent, "Devil's Backbone" is Granny's story.

As for the other characters in the feud: Devil Anse was as good as his word. He never again took up arms against his fellow man, though he was ever ready to go bear hunting. He was born again as a Christian following a revival meeting in 1911 and was baptized shortly thereafter.

The feud itself, was not nearly as constant as it appeared in "Devil's Backbone." As Granny said, there were lots of times when years would go by and nothing but nothing would happen. But that does not make for exciting reading.

As for the popular portrayals of the combating families as imbeciles who did not know what they were fighting over, nothing could be further from the truth. Grievances were deep and long-lived it is true, but there were legitimate reasons for the feud that festered for two generations and caused so much pain to both families. The Hatfield clan became a West Virginia success story. Devil Anse died in 1921, a prosperous farmer and former school superintendent who supplemented his income with timbering and royalties from coal mining. He had nine sons: Johnse, the eldest became a land agent for the US Steel Coal and Coke Company. Cap, his second son, while incarcerated, was pardoned for saving the life of the Lt. Governor who was attacked by an inmate during a tour of the prison. He studied law and practiced with his son and daughter, who was the first female lawyer in Logan County. Robert E. Lee became a rich property merchant. Elliot studied medicine and graduated from college in Louisville in 1898. Joe was elected High Sheriff of Logan County. So was his younger brother Tennis. By the way, Cap then served as deputy to them both. Willis became a personnel officer for a mining company. The only tragedy to strike this illustrious family was the murder of Elias and Troy by a disgruntled Italian restaurant owner.

Success was not limited to Devil Anse's immediate family. His brother Elias fathered Greenway, who was elected sheriff of Mingo County three times, Elias Jr., who became a doctor, and Henry, who as another doctor owned a large hospital in Huntington. The author himself was once patched up in the Hatfield hospital as a young boy, following a collision with some glass panes. Later in his life Henry was elected governor of West Virginia and then to the US Senate.

Well over a century has passed since the feud ended. Yet the story of the Hatfield – McCoy feud is etched in the American psyche. The tale as I relate it is a work of fiction as it would have been seen through my Granny Sally's colored glasses, had she worn glasses.

Acknowledgment

Thanks to Dennis Kutz and Tuff
and special thanks to John Harris for the
photo of See Bird used on the back cover.